Sir Arthur Conan Doyle's
The Adventure of
Wisteria Lodge

Adapted by: Vincent Goodwin

Illustrated by: Ben Dunn

magic
wagon

visit us at
www.abdopublishing.com

Published by Magic Wagon, a division of the ABDO Group, PO Box 398166, Minneapolis, MN, 55439.

Printed in the United States of America, North Mankato, Minnesota.
022012
092012
This book contains at least 10% recycled materials.

Written by Sir Arthur Conan Doyle
Adapted by Vincent Goodwin
Illustrated by Ben Dunn
Colored by Robby Bevard
Lettered by Doug Dlin
Edited by Stephanie Hedlund and Rochelle Baltzer
Interior layout by Antarctic Press
Cover art by Ben Dunn
Cover design by Abbey Fitzgerald

Library of Congress Cataloging-in-Publication Data

Goodwin, Vincent.
Sir Arthur Conan Doyle's The adventure of Wisteria Lodge / adapted by Vincent Goodwin ; illustrated by Ben Dunn.
p. cm. -- (The graphic novel adventures of Sherlock Holmes)
Summary: Retold in graphic novel form, Sherlock Holmes investigates a baffling case of a murder involving a foreign tyrant, a governess, and a tale of revenge.
ISBN 978-1-61641-896-0
1. Doyle, Arthur Conan, Sir, 1859-1930. Adventure of Wisteria Lodge--Adaptations. 2. Holmes, Sherlock (Fictitious character)--Comic books, strips, etc. 3. Holmes, Sherlock (Fictitious character)--Juvenile fiction. 4. Graphic novels. [1. Graphic novels. 2. Doyle, Arthur Conan, Sir, 1859-1930. Adventure of Wisteria Lodge--Adaptations. 3. Mystery and detective stories.] I. Dunn, Ben, ill. II. Doyle, Arthur Conan, Sir, 1859-1930. Adventure of Wisteria Lodge. III. Title. IV. Title: Adventure of Wisteria Lodge. V. Series: Goodwin, Vincent. Graphic novel adventures of Sherlock Holmes.
PZ7.7.G66Siw 2012
741.5'973--dc23

2011052269

Table of Contents

Cast

Sherlock Holmes

Dr. John Watson

Mr. Aloysius Garcia

Mr. Scott Eccles

The Cook

Mr. Melville

Inspector Baynes

Miss Burnet

Don Murillo, AKA Mr. Henderson

Mr. Lucas

4

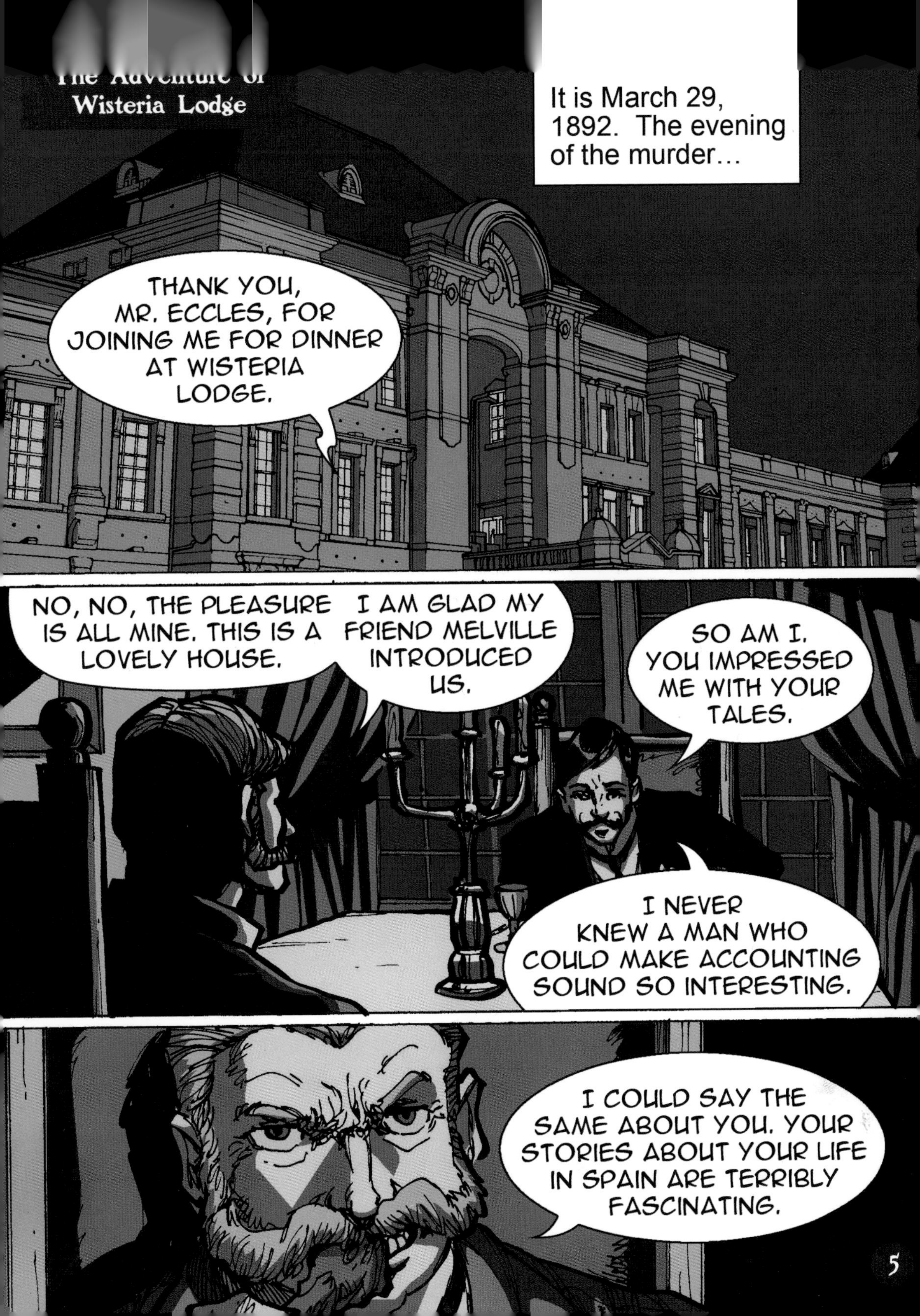
It is March 29, 1892. The evening of the murder…
THANK YOU, MR. ECCLES, FOR JOINING ME FOR DINNER AT WISTERIA LODGE.
NO, NO, THE PLEASURE IS ALL MINE. THIS IS A LOVELY HOUSE.
I AM GLAD MY FRIEND MELVILLE INTRODUCED US.
SO AM I. YOU IMPRESSED ME WITH YOUR TALES.
I NEVER KNEW A MAN WHO COULD MAKE ACCOUNTING SOUND SO INTERESTING.
I COULD SAY THE SAME ABOUT YOU. YOUR STORIES ABOUT YOUR LIFE IN SPAIN ARE TERRIBLY FASCINATING.

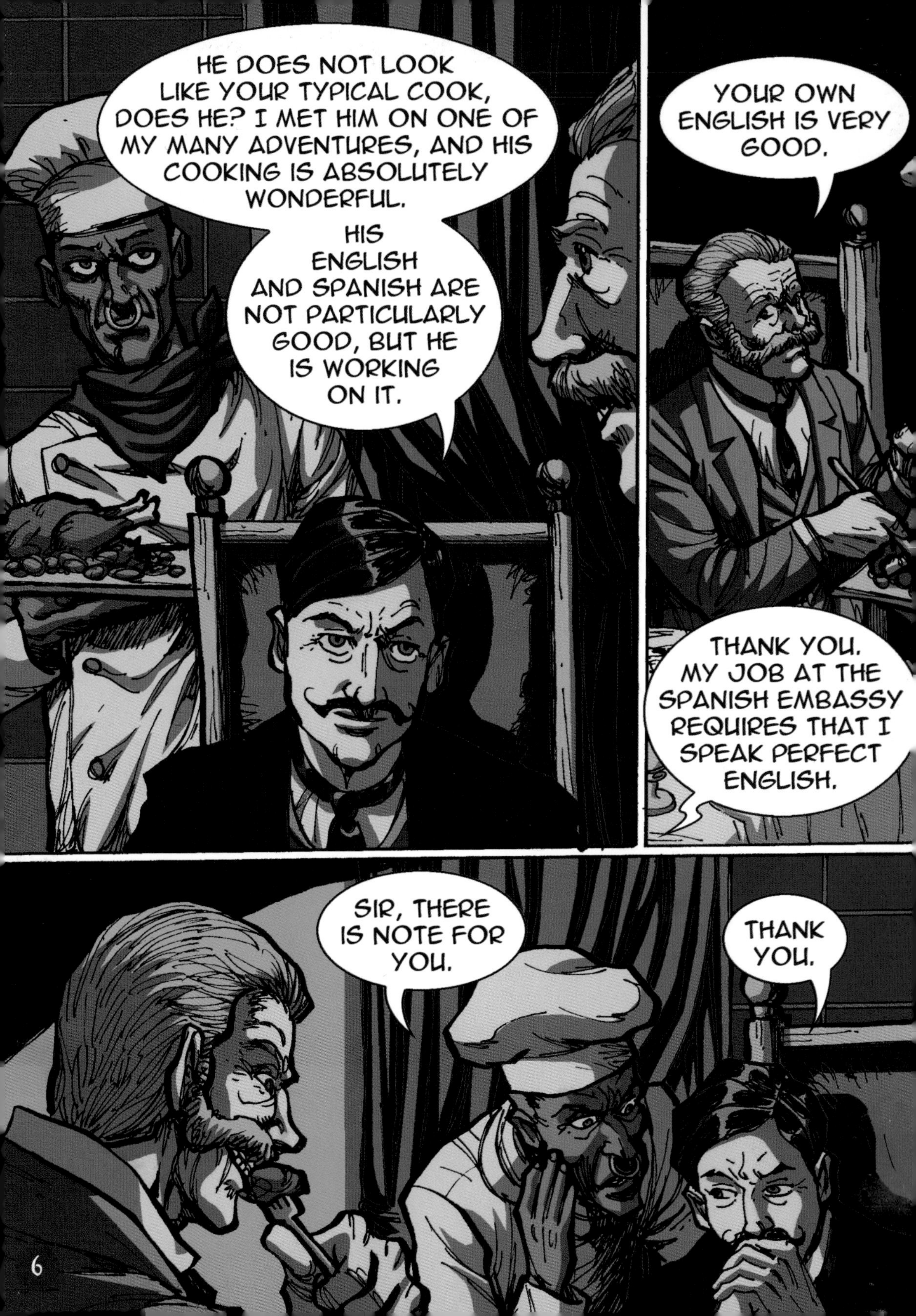
HE DOES NOT LOOK LIKE YOUR TYPICAL COOK, DOES HE? I MET HIM ON ONE OF MY MANY ADVENTURES, AND HIS COOKING IS ABSOLUTELY WONDERFUL.
HIS ENGLISH AND SPANISH ARE NOT PARTICULARLY GOOD, BUT HE IS WORKING ON IT.
YOUR OWN ENGLISH IS VERY GOOD.
THANK YOU. MY JOB AT THE SPANISH EMBASSY REQUIRES THAT I SPEAK PERFECT ENGLISH.
SIR, THERE IS NOTE FOR YOU.
THANK YOU.

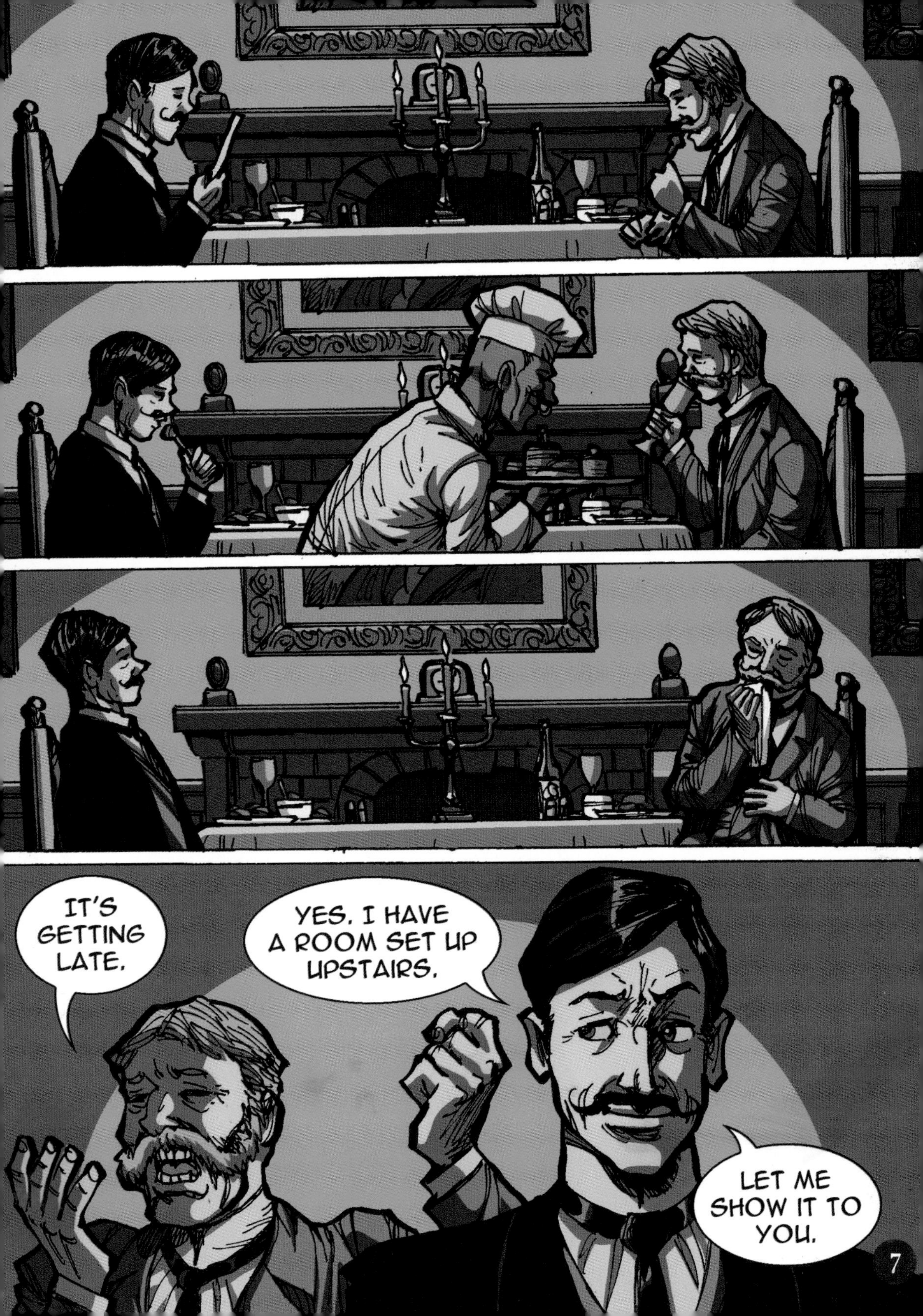
IT'S GETTING LATE.
YES. I HAVE A ROOM SET UP UPSTAIRS.
LET ME SHOW IT TO YOU.

In the middle of the night…

SCOTT? WERE YOU WANDERING ABOUT? I HEARD FOOTSTEPS.

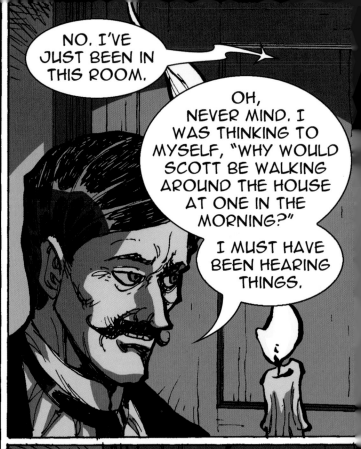

NO. I'VE JUST BEEN IN THIS ROOM.

OH, NEVER MIND. I WAS THINKING TO MYSELF, "WHY WOULD SCOTT BE WALKING AROUND THE HOUSE AT ONE IN THE MORNING?"

I MUST HAVE BEEN HEARING THINGS.

SORRY FOR DISTURBING YOU. GOOD NIGHT.

GOOD NIGHT.

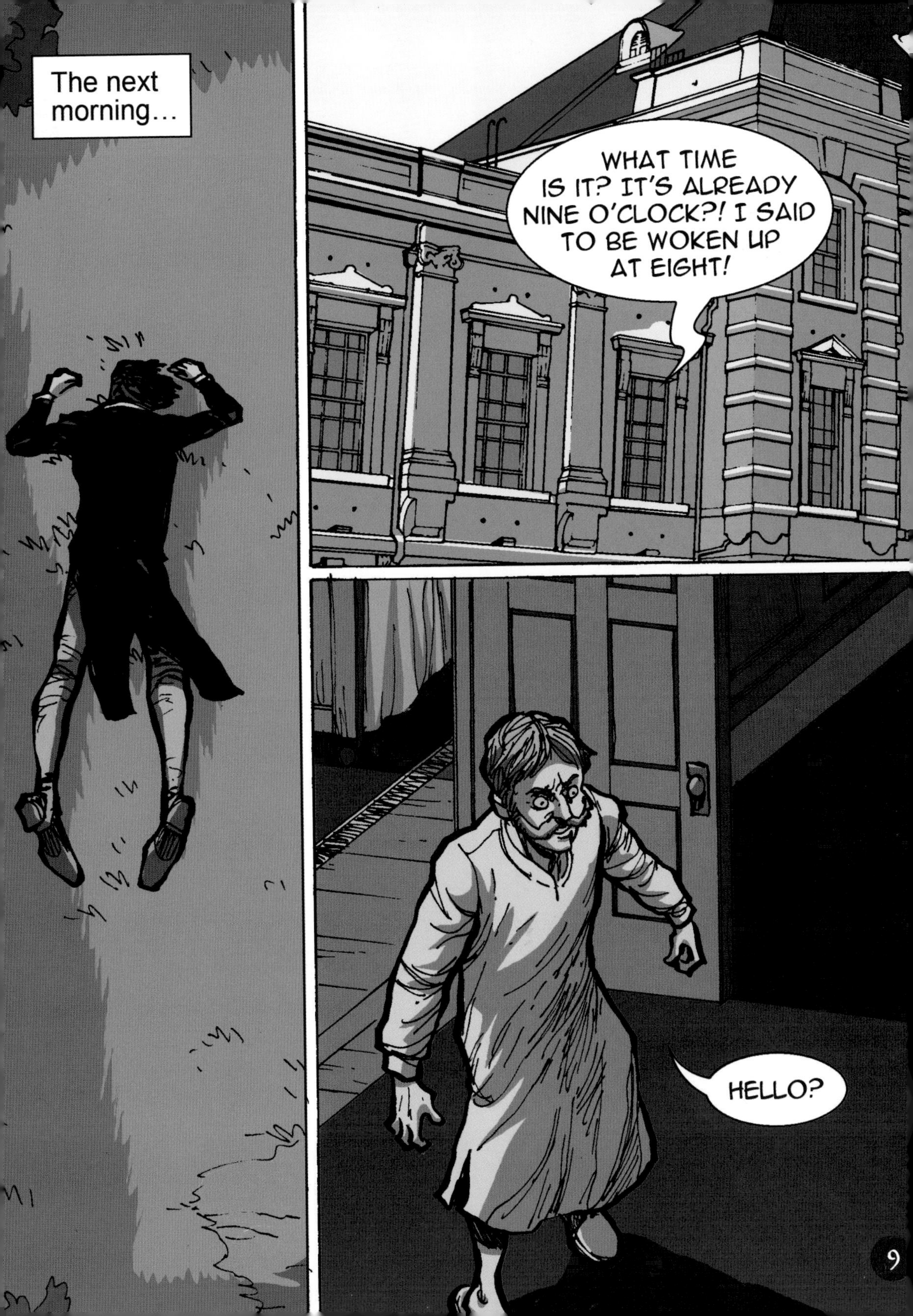
The next morning…
WHAT TIME IS IT? IT'S ALREADY NINE O'CLOCK?! I SAID TO BE WOKEN UP AT EIGHT!
HELLO?

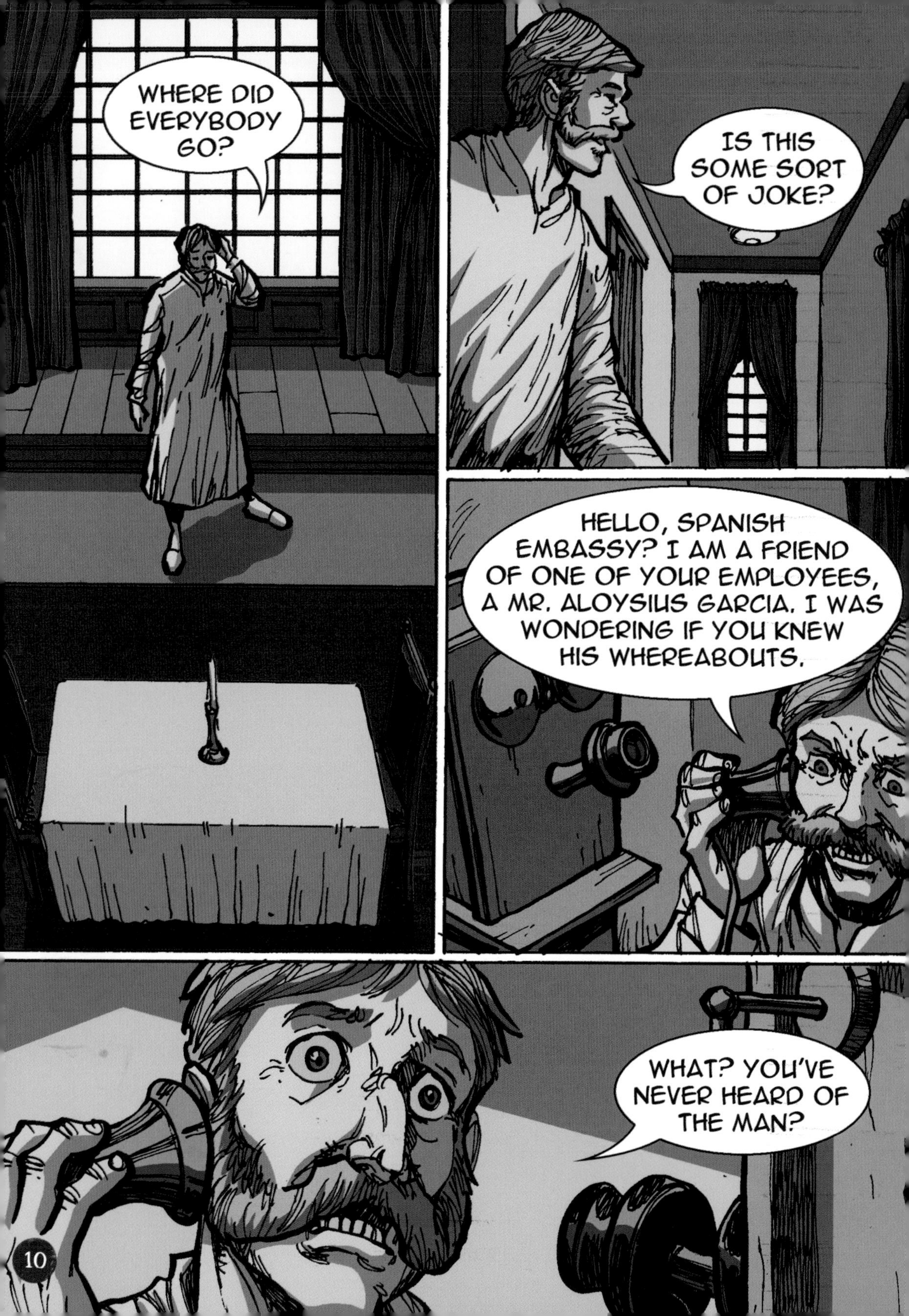
WHERE DID EVERYBODY GO?
IS THIS SOME SORT OF JOKE?
HELLO, SPANISH EMBASSY? I AM A FRIEND OF ONE OF YOUR EMPLOYEES, A MR. ALOYSIUS GARCIA. I WAS WONDERING IF YOU KNEW HIS WHEREABOUTS.
WHAT? YOU'VE NEVER HEARD OF THE MAN?

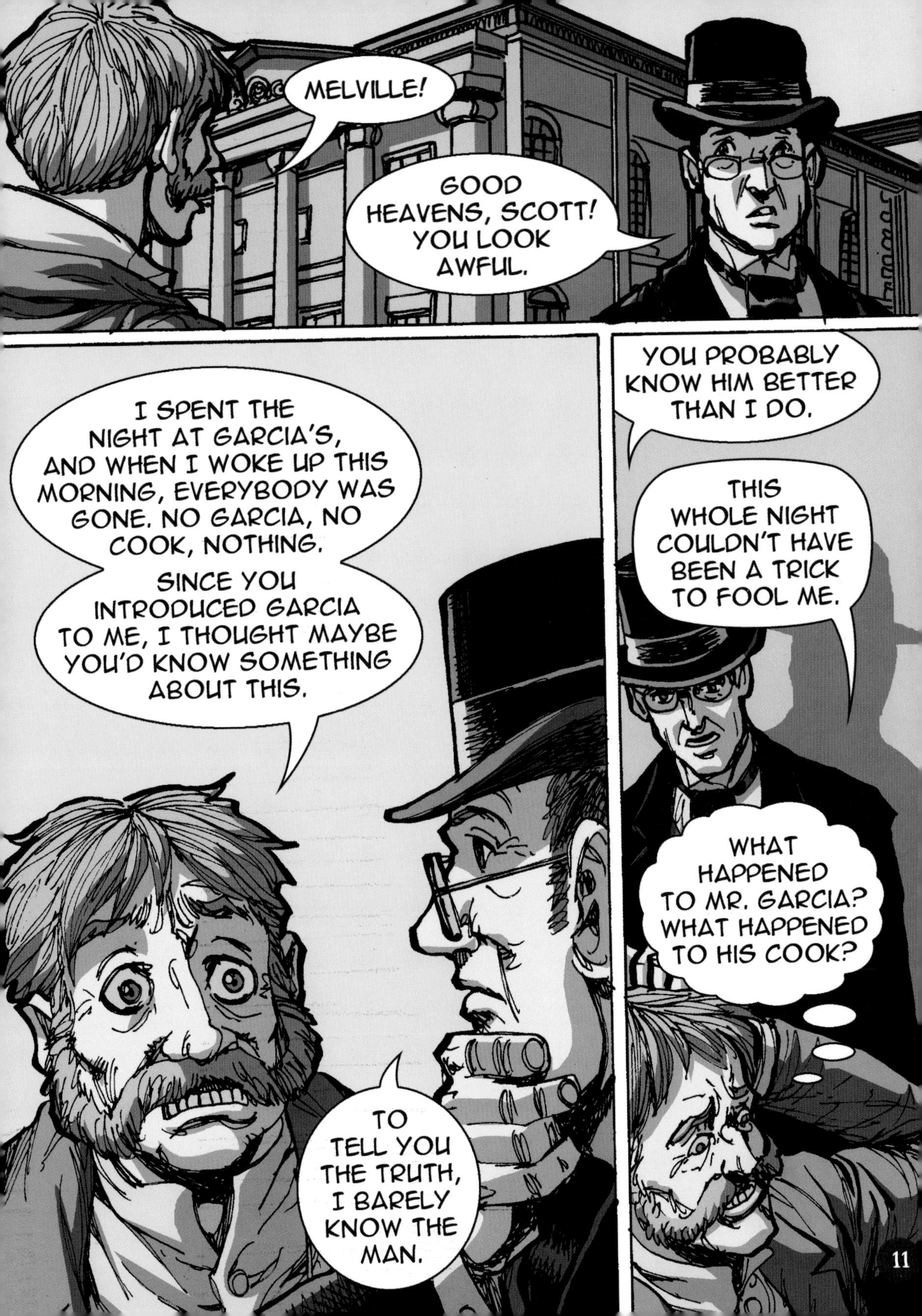
MELVILLE!
GOOD HEAVENS, SCOTT! YOU LOOK AWFUL.
I SPENT THE NIGHT AT GARCIA'S, AND WHEN I WOKE UP THIS MORNING, EVERYBODY WAS GONE. NO GARCIA, NO COOK, NOTHING.
SINCE YOU INTRODUCED GARCIA TO ME, I THOUGHT MAYBE YOU'D KNOW SOMETHING ABOUT THIS.
TO TELL YOU THE TRUTH, I BARELY KNOW THE MAN.
YOU PROBABLY KNOW HIM BETTER THAN I DO.
THIS WHOLE NIGHT COULDN'T HAVE BEEN A TRICK TO FOOL ME.
WHAT HAPPENED TO MR. GARCIA? WHAT HAPPENED TO HIS COOK?

Back at Wisteria Lodge, Sherlock Holmes and Dr. Watson join Inspector Baynes.

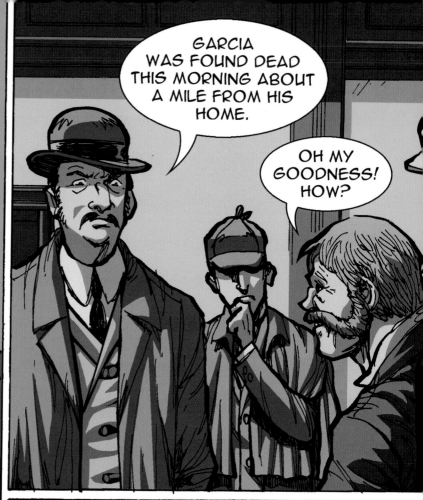

GARCIA WAS FOUND DEAD THIS MORNING ABOUT A MILE FROM HIS HOME.

OH MY GOODNESS! HOW?

HIS HEAD HAD BEEN SMASHED TO PULP.

POLI

THERE WAS A LETTER IN HIS POCKET. IT SAID, "OUR OWN COLORS, GREEN AND WHITE. GREEN OPEN, WHITE SHUT. MAIN STAIR, FIRST HALL, SEVENTH RIGHT, GREEN BAIZE. GODSPEED. D."
DO YOU KNOW WHAT THAT MEANS?
I'M SORRY, I DON'T.
THE HANDWRITING LOOKS LIKE IT'S FROM A WOMAN.
BUT THE ADDRESS IS EITHER DONE WITH ANOTHER PEN OR BY SOMEONE ELSE. IT IS THICKER AND BOLDER.
INSPECTOR BAYNES, DO YOU KNOW THE TIME OF DEATH?
ABOUT ONE IN THE MORNING.
THERE WAS RAIN ABOUT THAT TIME, AND THE BODY HAD CERTAINLY BEEN HERE BEFORE THE RAIN.
THAT'S IMPOSSIBLE. I TALKED TO HIM AT ONE. HE SAID, "WHY WOULD SCOTT BE WALKING AROUND THE HOUSE AT ONE IN THE MORNING?"
THAT'S ODD, BUT BY NO MEANS IMPOSSIBLE.

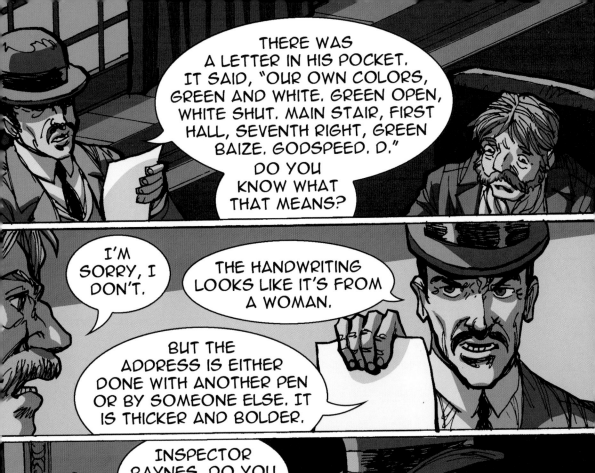

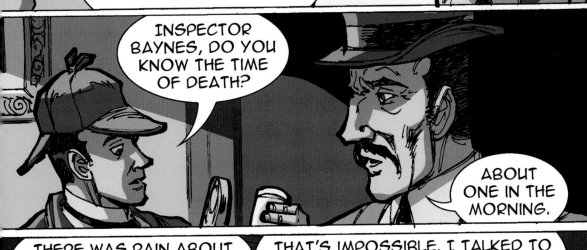

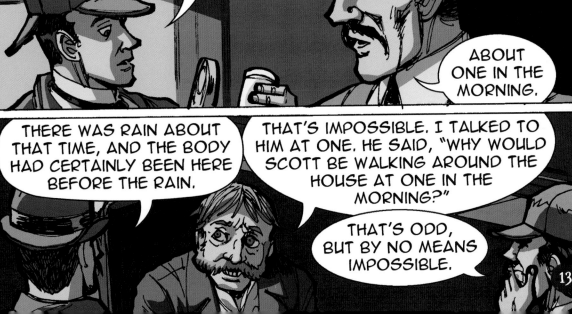

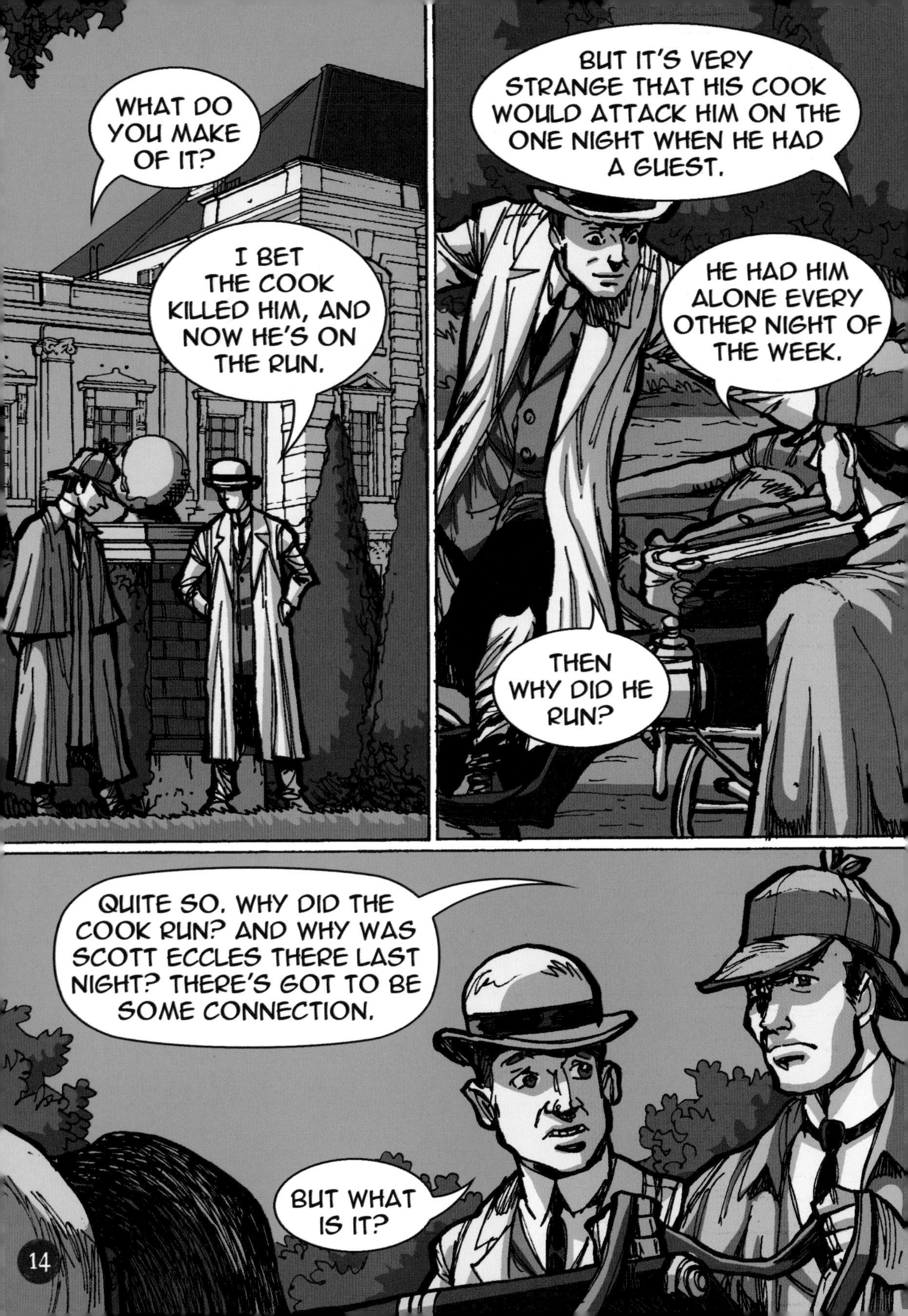
WHAT DO YOU MAKE OF IT?
I BET THE COOK KILLED HIM, AND NOW HE'S ON THE RUN.
BUT IT'S VERY STRANGE THAT HIS COOK WOULD ATTACK HIM ON THE ONE NIGHT WHEN HE HAD A GUEST.
HE HAD HIM ALONE EVERY OTHER NIGHT OF THE WEEK.
THEN WHY DID HE RUN?
QUITE SO. WHY DID THE COOK RUN? AND WHY WAS SCOTT ECCLES THERE LAST NIGHT? THERE'S GOT TO BE SOME CONNECTION.
BUT WHAT IS IT?

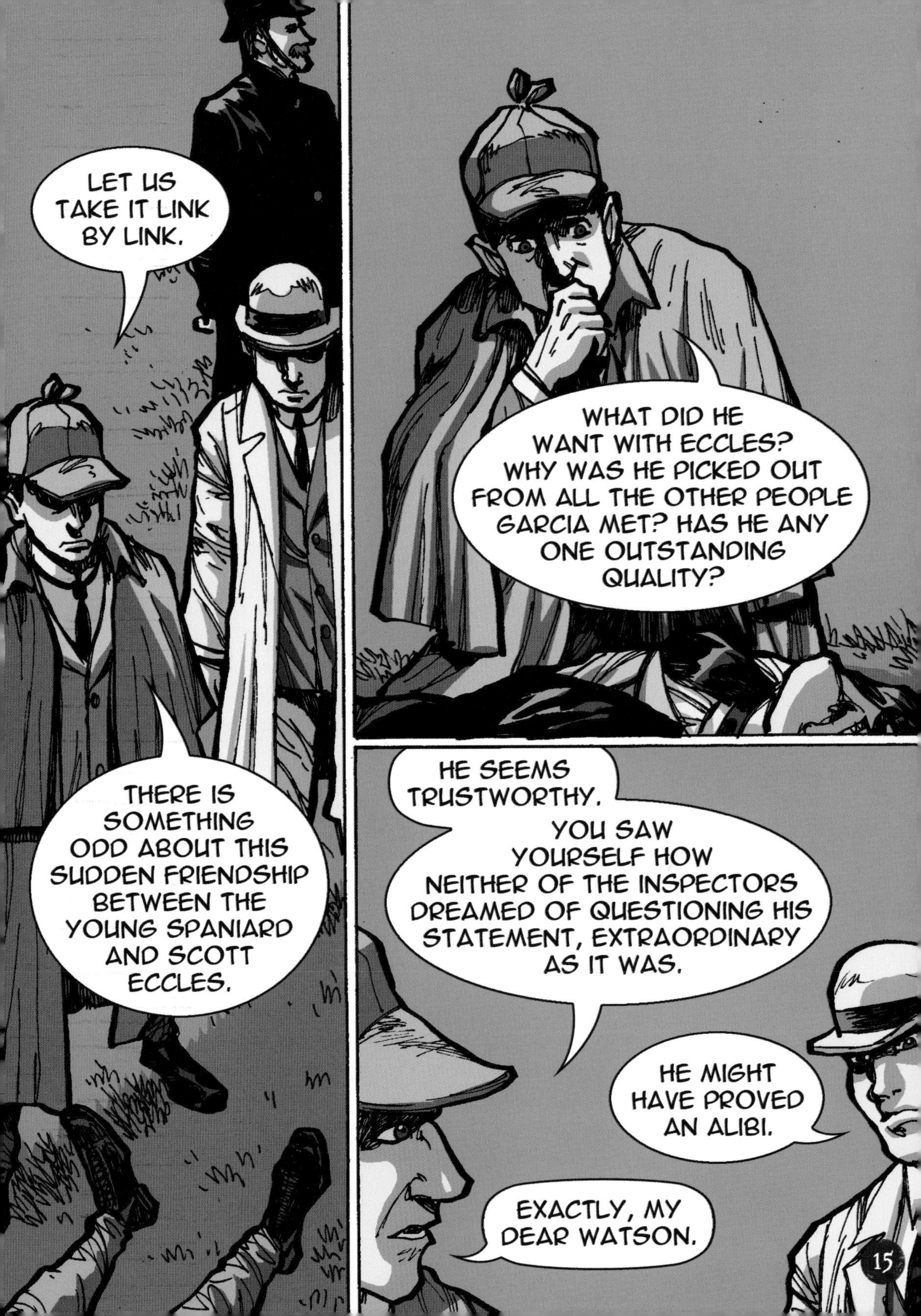
LET US TAKE IT LINK BY LINK.
THERE IS SOMETHING ODD ABOUT THIS SUDDEN FRIENDSHIP BETWEEN THE YOUNG SPANIARD AND SCOTT ECCLES.
WHAT DID HE WANT WITH ECCLES? WHY WAS HE PICKED OUT FROM ALL THE OTHER PEOPLE GARCIA MET? HAS HE ANY ONE OUTSTANDING QUALITY?
HE SEEMS TRUSTWORTHY.
YOU SAW YOURSELF HOW NEITHER OF THE INSPECTORS DREAMED OF QUESTIONING HIS STATEMENT, EXTRAORDINARY AS IT WAS.
HE MIGHT HAVE PROVED AN ALIBI.
EXACTLY, MY DEAR WATSON.

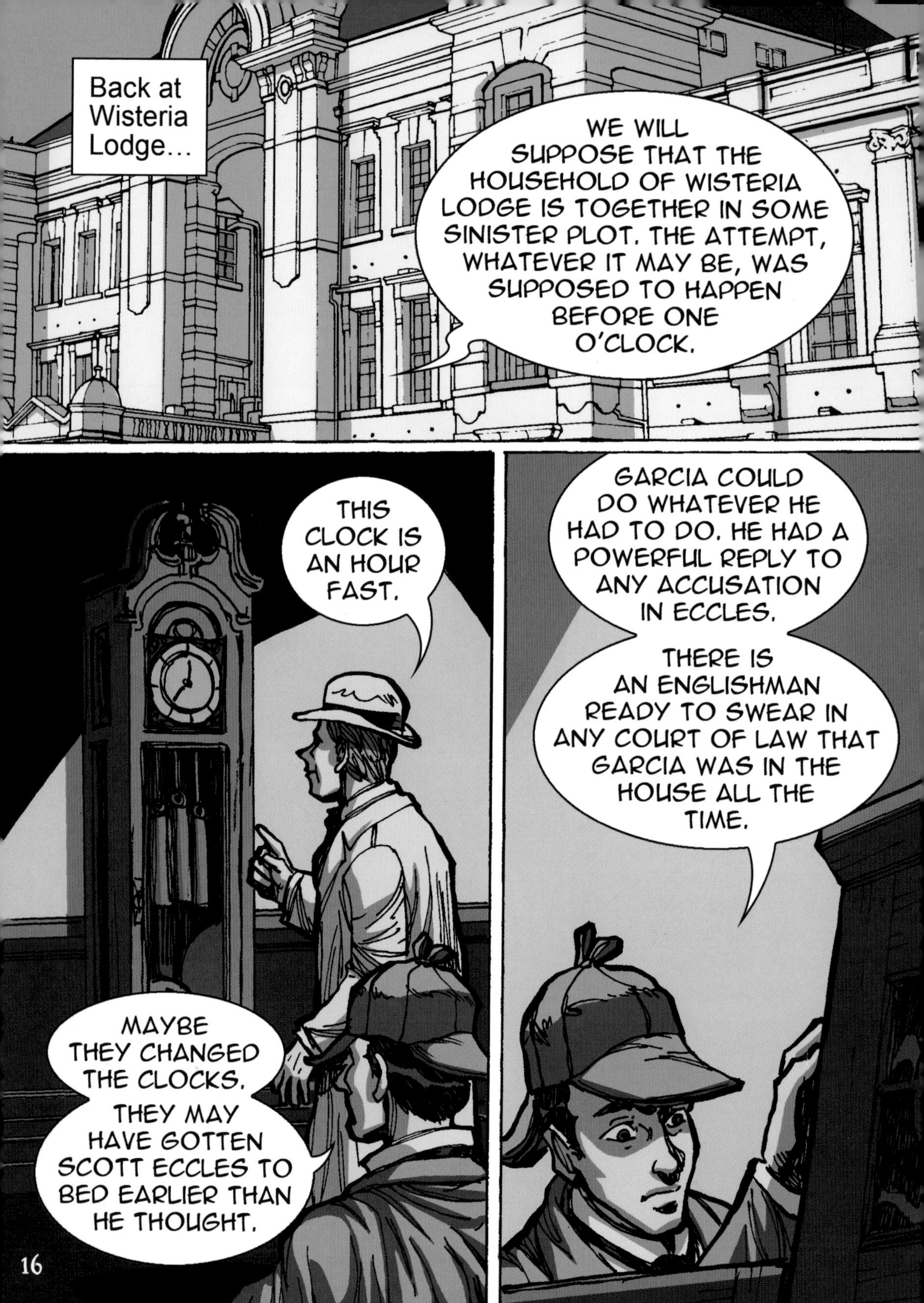

Back at Wisteria Lodge…
WE WILL SUPPOSE THAT THE HOUSEHOLD OF WISTERIA LODGE IS TOGETHER IN SOME SINISTER PLOT. THE ATTEMPT, WHATEVER IT MAY BE, WAS SUPPOSED TO HAPPEN BEFORE ONE O'CLOCK.
THIS CLOCK IS AN HOUR FAST.
MAYBE THEY CHANGED THE CLOCKS.
THEY MAY HAVE GOTTEN SCOTT ECCLES TO BED EARLIER THAN HE THOUGHT.
GARCIA COULD DO WHATEVER HE HAD TO DO. HE HAD A POWERFUL REPLY TO ANY ACCUSATION IN ECCLES.
THERE IS AN ENGLISHMAN READY TO SWEAR IN ANY COURT OF LAW THAT GARCIA WAS IN THE HOUSE ALL THE TIME.

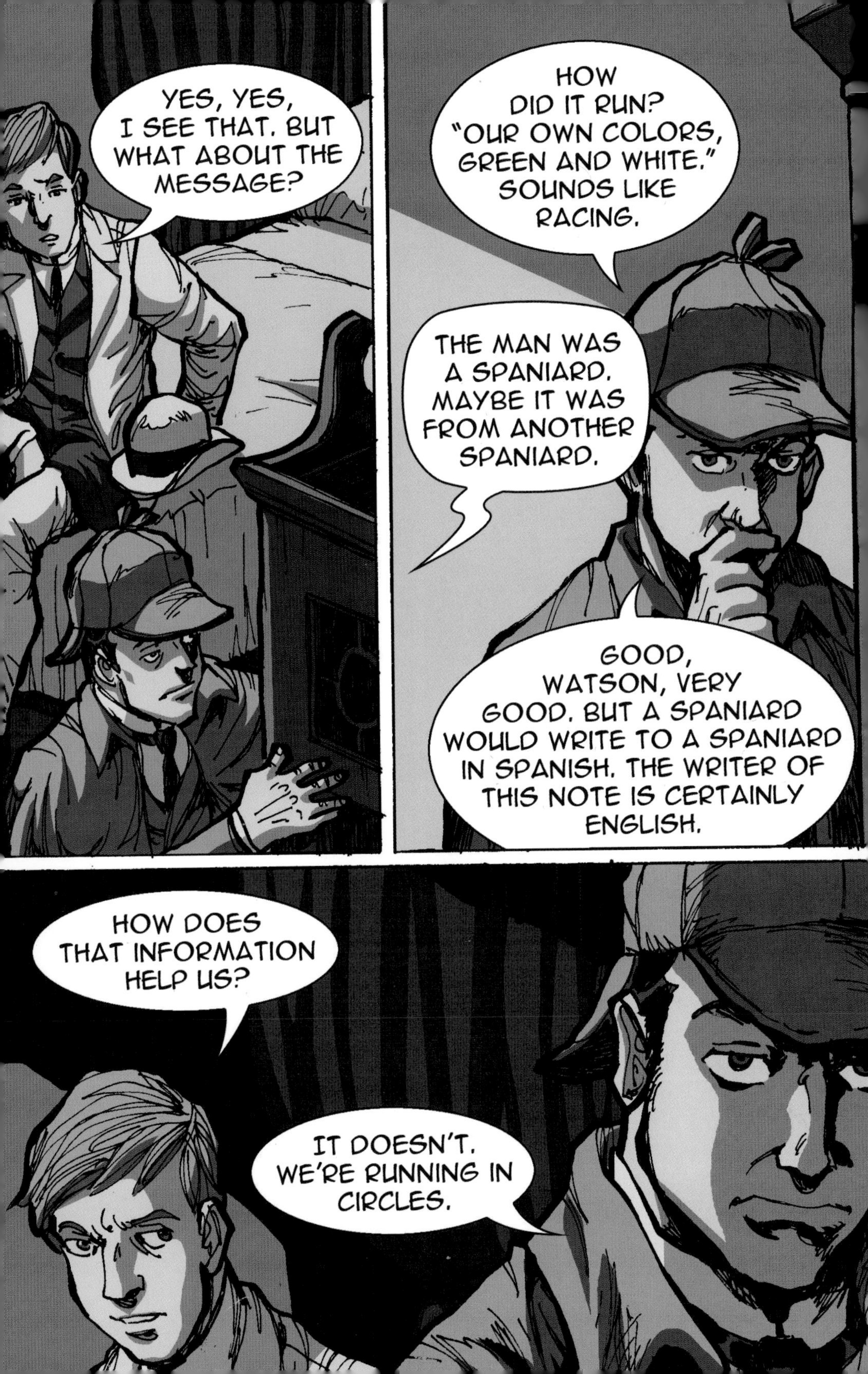
YES, YES, I SEE THAT. BUT WHAT ABOUT THE MESSAGE?
HOW DID IT RUN? "OUR OWN COLORS, GREEN AND WHITE." SOUNDS LIKE RACING.
THE MAN WAS A SPANIARD. MAYBE IT WAS FROM ANOTHER SPANIARD.
GOOD, WATSON, VERY GOOD. BUT A SPANIARD WOULD WRITE TO A SPANIARD IN SPANISH. THE WRITER OF THIS NOTE IS CERTAINLY ENGLISH.
HOW DOES THAT INFORMATION HELP US?
IT DOESN'T. WE'RE RUNNING IN CIRCLES.

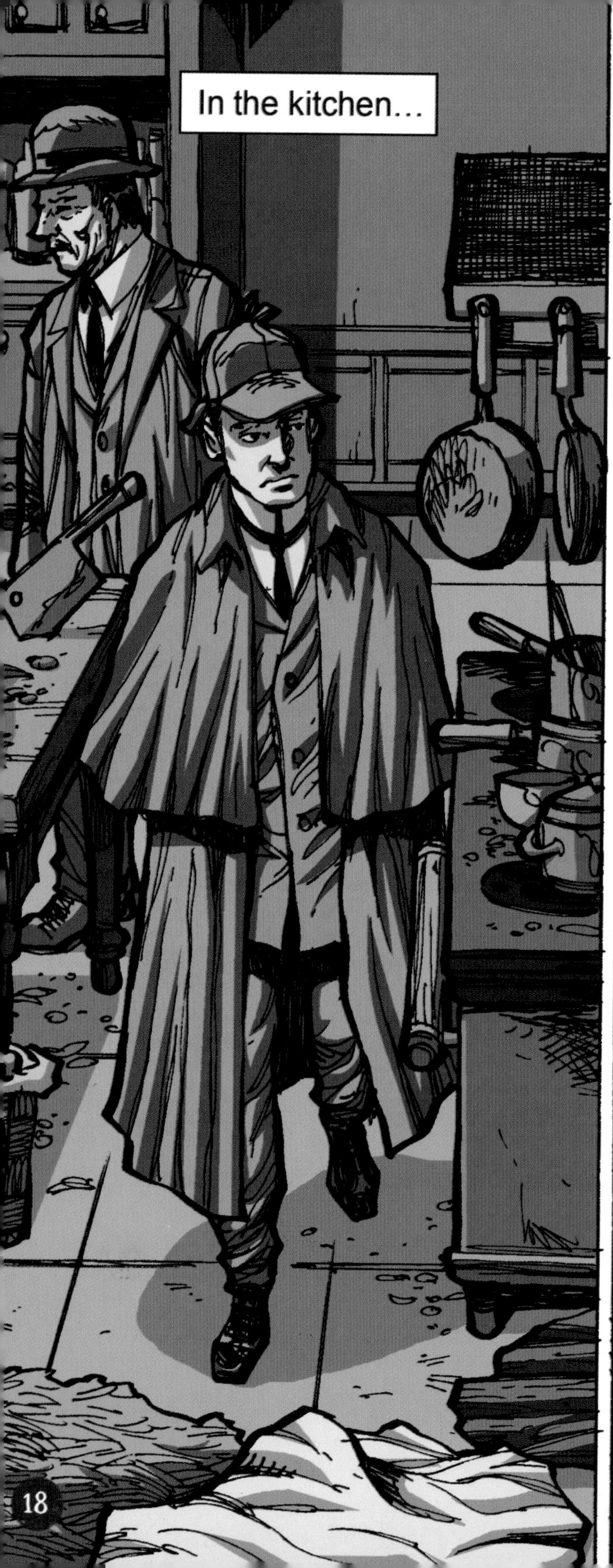
In the kitchen…

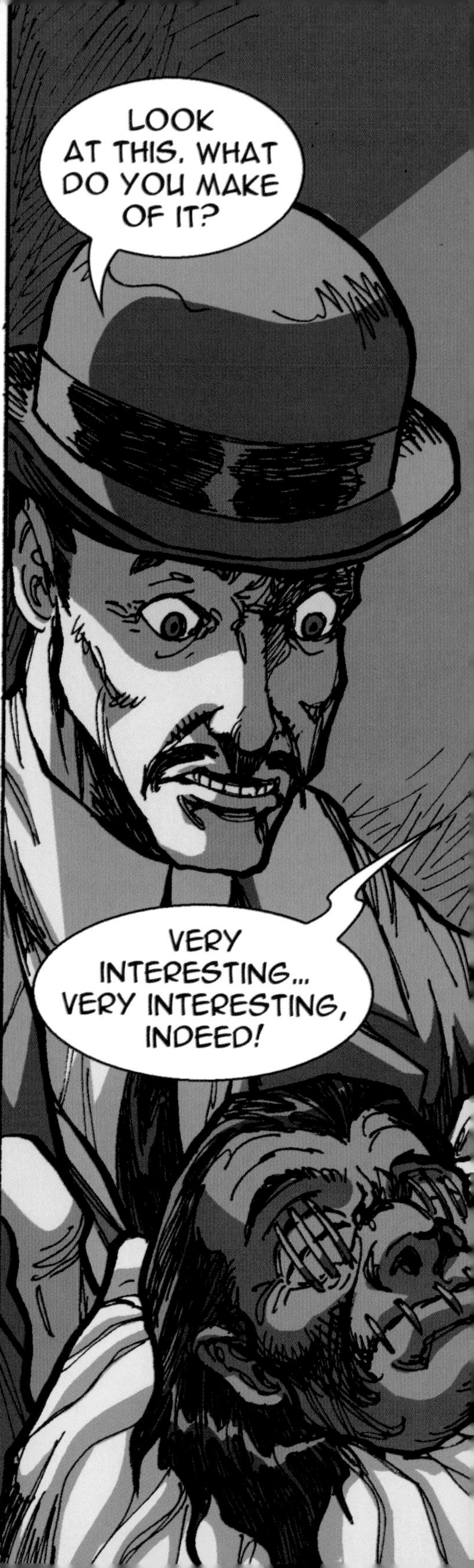
LOOK AT THIS. WHAT DO YOU MAKE OF IT?
VERY INTERESTING… VERY INTERESTING, INDEED!

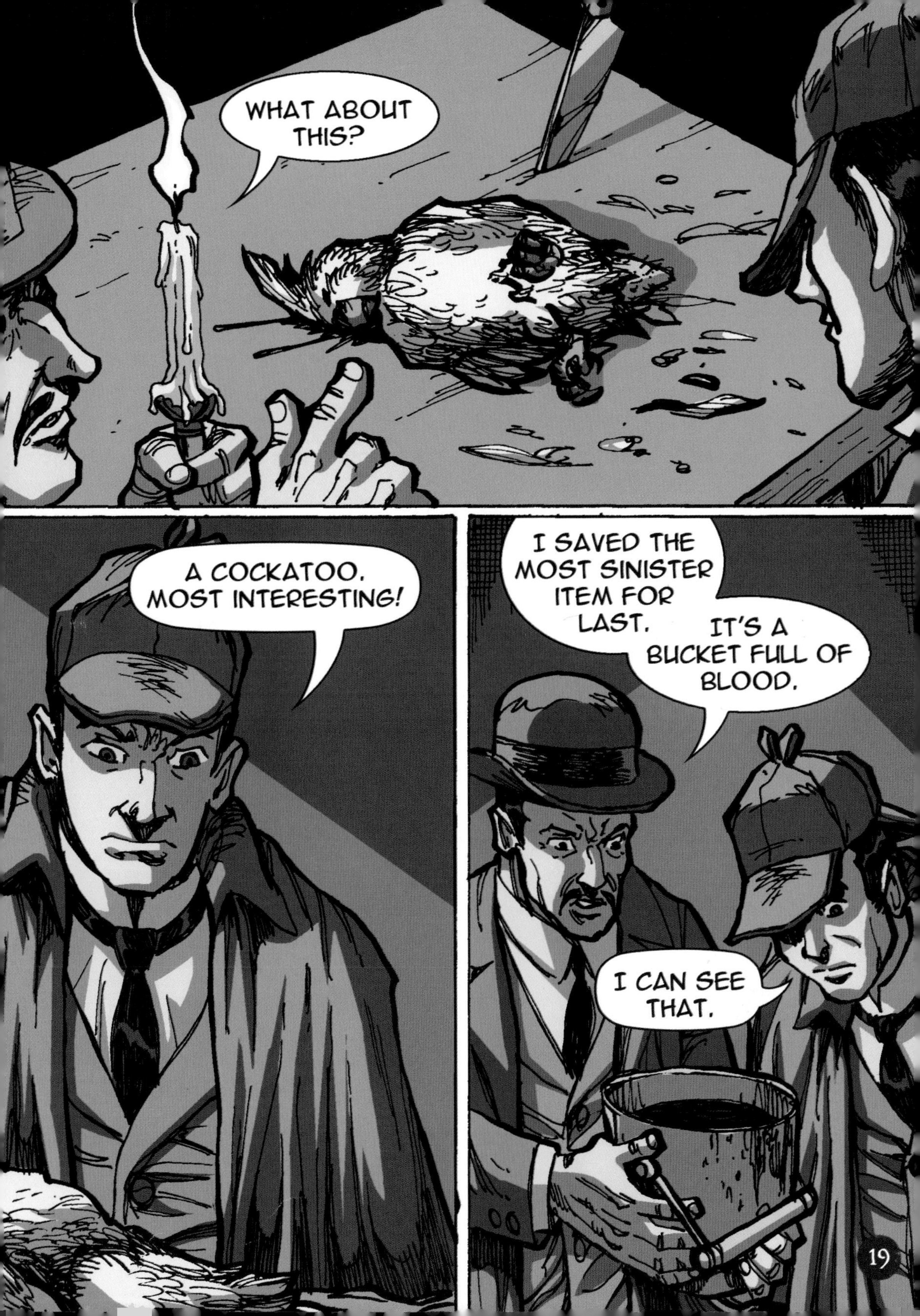
WHAT ABOUT THIS?
A COCKATOO. MOST INTERESTING!
I SAVED THE MOST SINISTER ITEM FOR LAST.
IT'S A BUCKET FULL OF BLOOD.
I CAN SEE THAT.

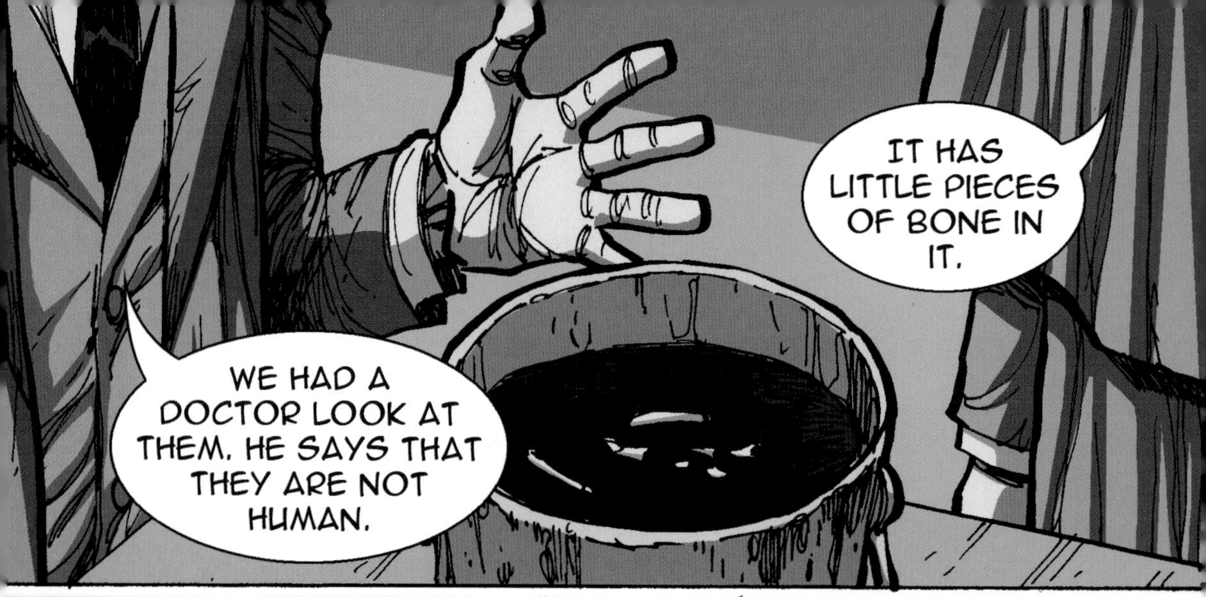
IT HAS LITTLE PIECES OF BONE IN IT.
WE HAD A DOCTOR LOOK AT THEM. HE SAYS THAT THEY ARE NOT HUMAN.

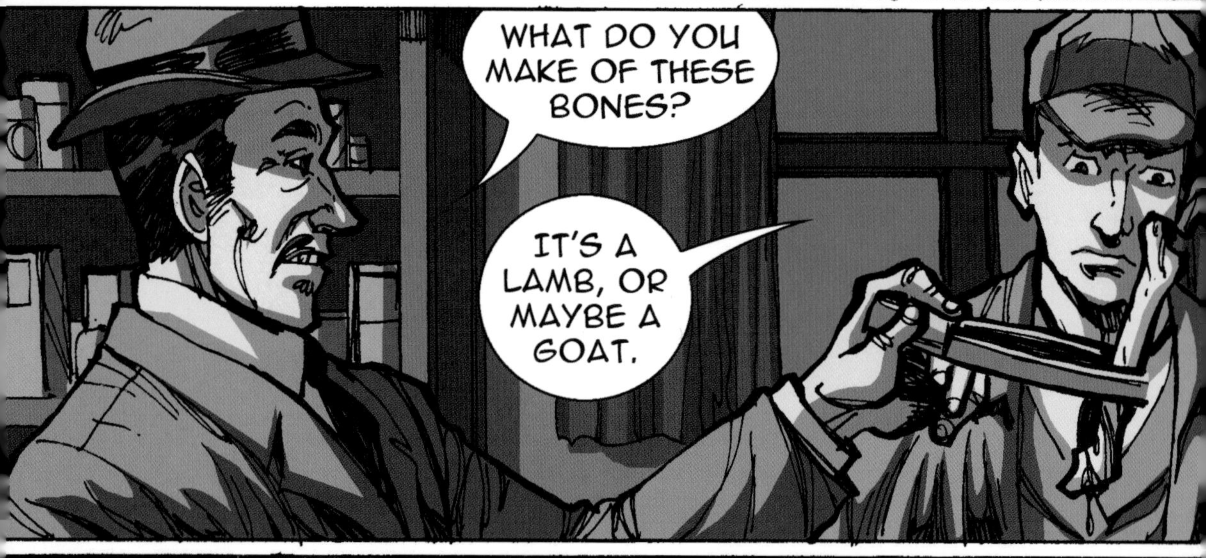
WHAT DO YOU MAKE OF THESE BONES?
IT'S A LAMB, OR MAYBE A GOAT.

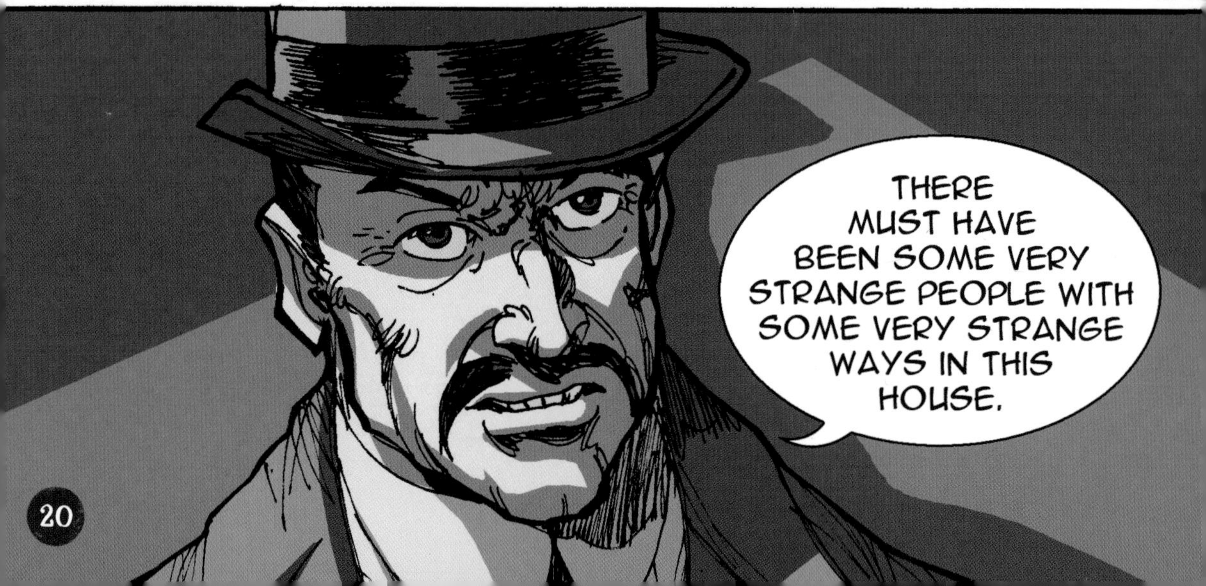
THERE MUST HAVE BEEN SOME VERY STRANGE PEOPLE WITH SOME VERY STRANGE WAYS IN THIS HOUSE.

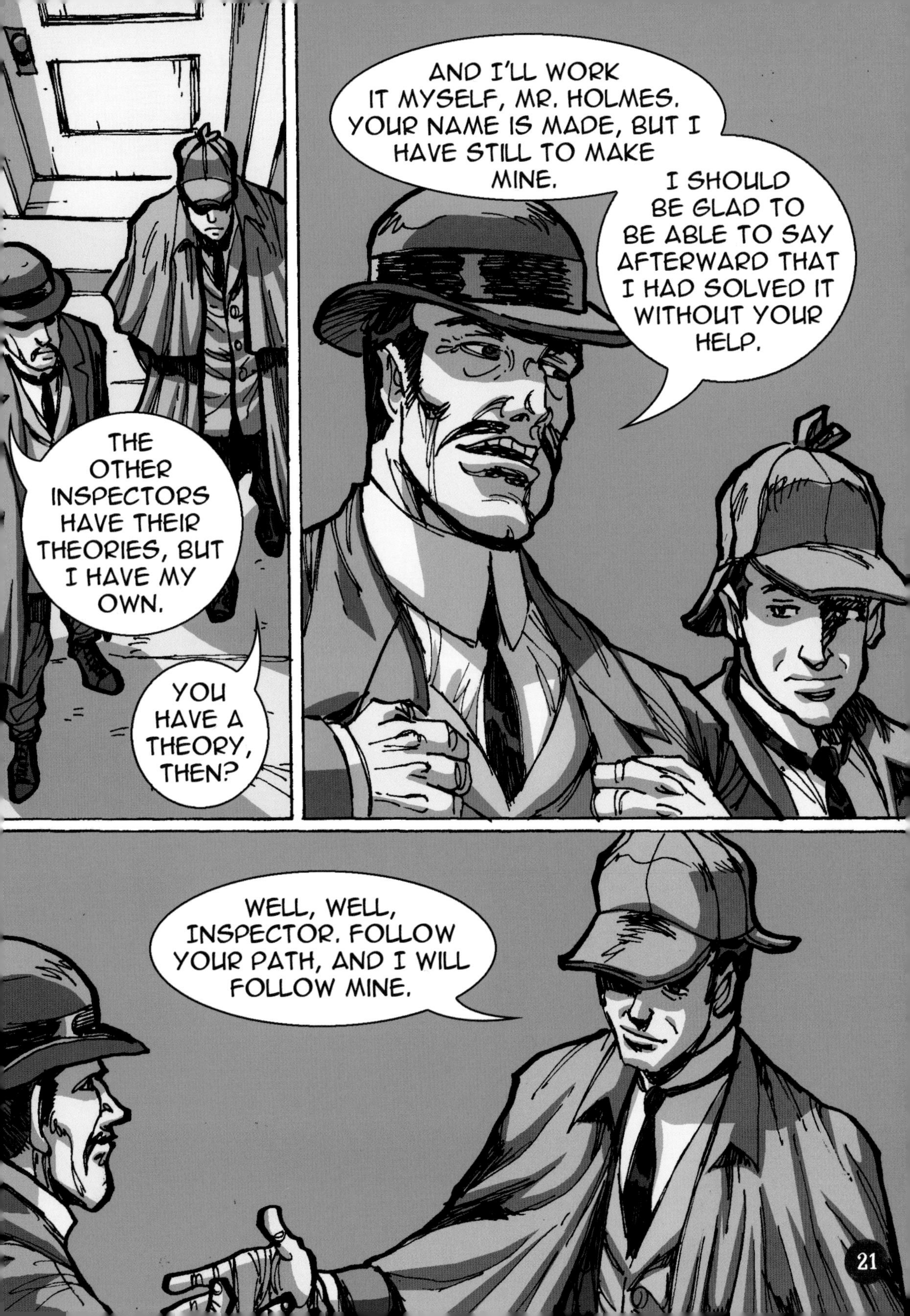
THE OTHER INSPECTORS HAVE THEIR THEORIES, BUT I HAVE MY OWN.
YOU HAVE A THEORY, THEN?
AND I'LL WORK IT MYSELF, MR. HOLMES. YOUR NAME IS MADE, BUT I HAVE STILL TO MAKE MINE.
I SHOULD BE GLAD TO BE ABLE TO SAY AFTERWARD THAT I HAD SOLVED IT WITHOUT YOUR HELP.
WELL, WELL, INSPECTOR. FOLLOW YOUR PATH, AND I WILL FOLLOW MINE.

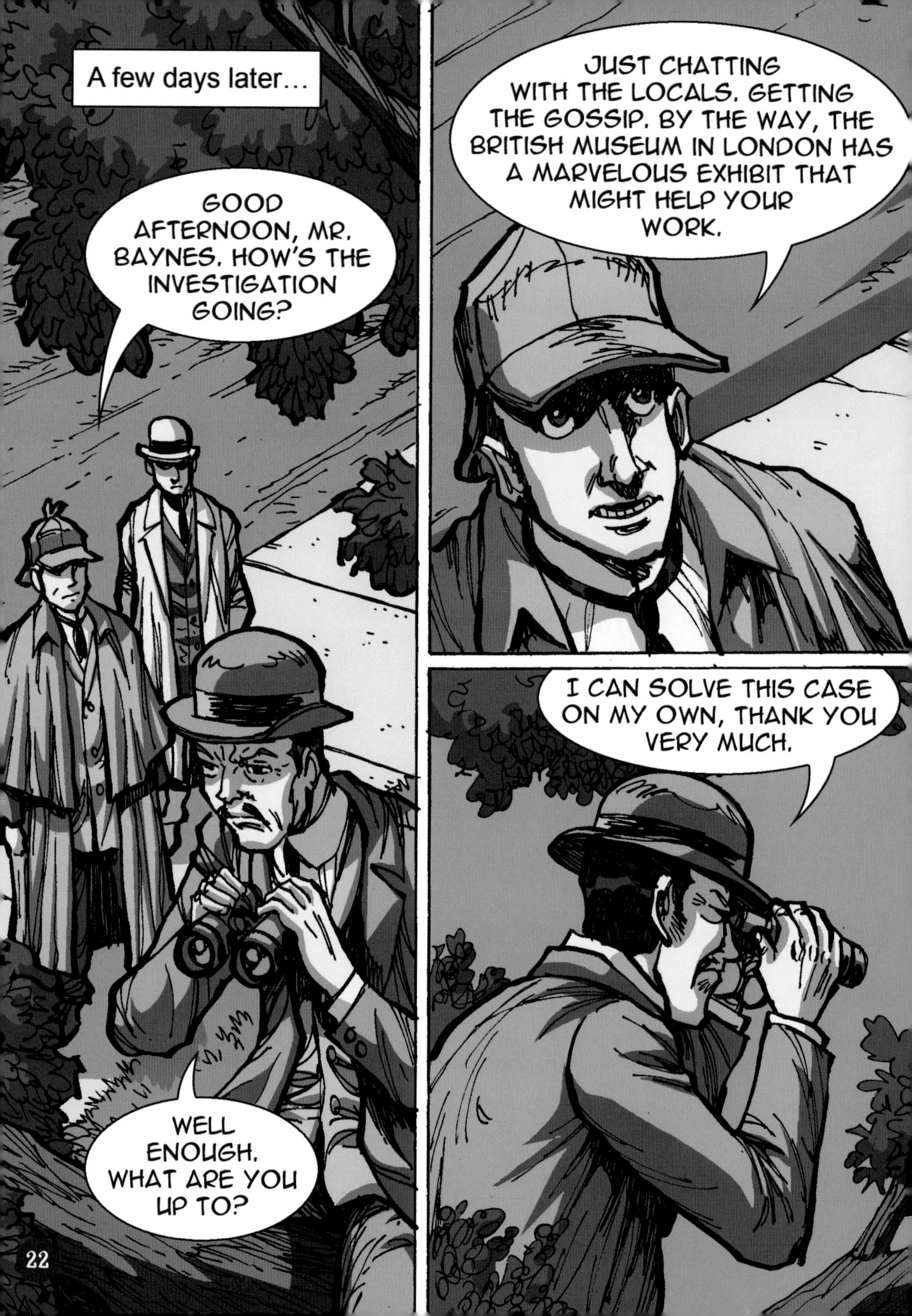
A few days later…
GOOD AFTERNOON, MR. BAYNES. HOW'S THE INVESTIGATION GOING?
WELL ENOUGH. WHAT ARE YOU UP TO?
JUST CHATTING WITH THE LOCALS. GETTING THE GOSSIP. BY THE WAY, THE BRITISH MUSEUM IN LONDON HAS A MARVELOUS EXHIBIT THAT MIGHT HELP YOUR WORK.
I CAN SOLVE THIS CASE ON MY OWN, THANK YOU VERY MUCH.

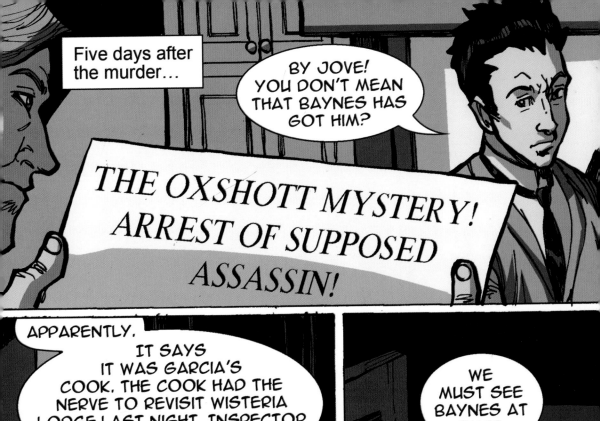

Five days after the murder…

BY JOVE! YOU DON'T MEAN THAT BAYNES HAS GOT HIM?

THE OXSHOTT MYSTERY! ARREST OF SUPPOSED ASSASSIN!

APPARENTLY.

IT SAYS IT WAS GARCIA'S COOK. THE COOK HAD THE NERVE TO REVISIT WISTERIA LODGE LAST NIGHT. INSPECTOR BAYNES WAS THERE TO AMBUSH HIM.

WE MUST SEE BAYNES AT ONCE.

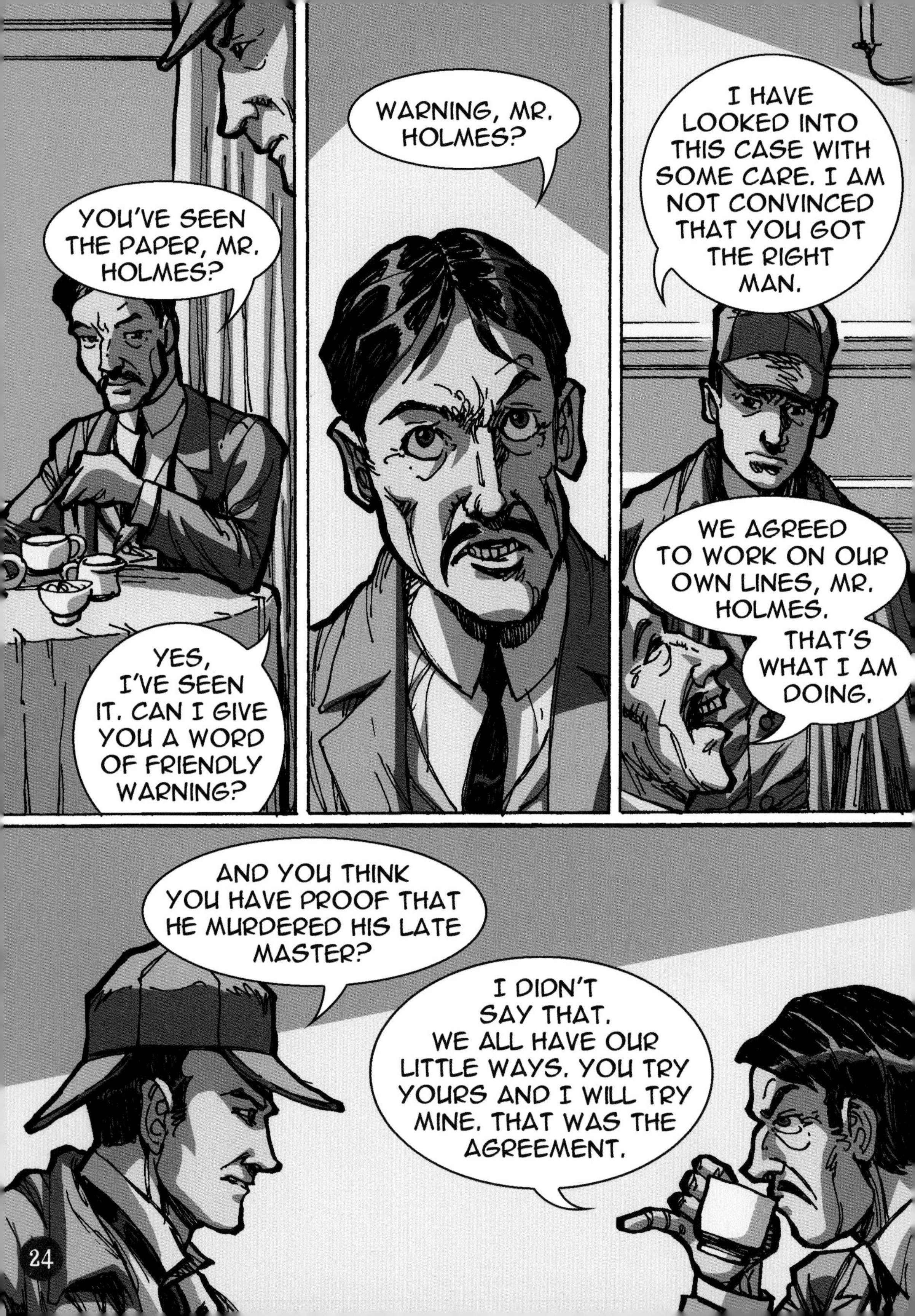
YOU'VE SEEN THE PAPER, MR. HOLMES?
YES, I'VE SEEN IT. CAN I GIVE YOU A WORD OF FRIENDLY WARNING?
WARNING, MR. HOLMES?
I HAVE LOOKED INTO THIS CASE WITH SOME CARE. I AM NOT CONVINCED THAT YOU GOT THE RIGHT MAN.
WE AGREED TO WORK ON OUR OWN LINES, MR. HOLMES.
THAT'S WHAT I AM DOING.
AND YOU THINK YOU HAVE PROOF THAT HE MURDERED HIS LATE MASTER?
I DIDN'T SAY THAT. WE ALL HAVE OUR LITTLE WAYS. YOU TRY YOURS AND I WILL TRY MINE. THAT WAS THE AGREEMENT.

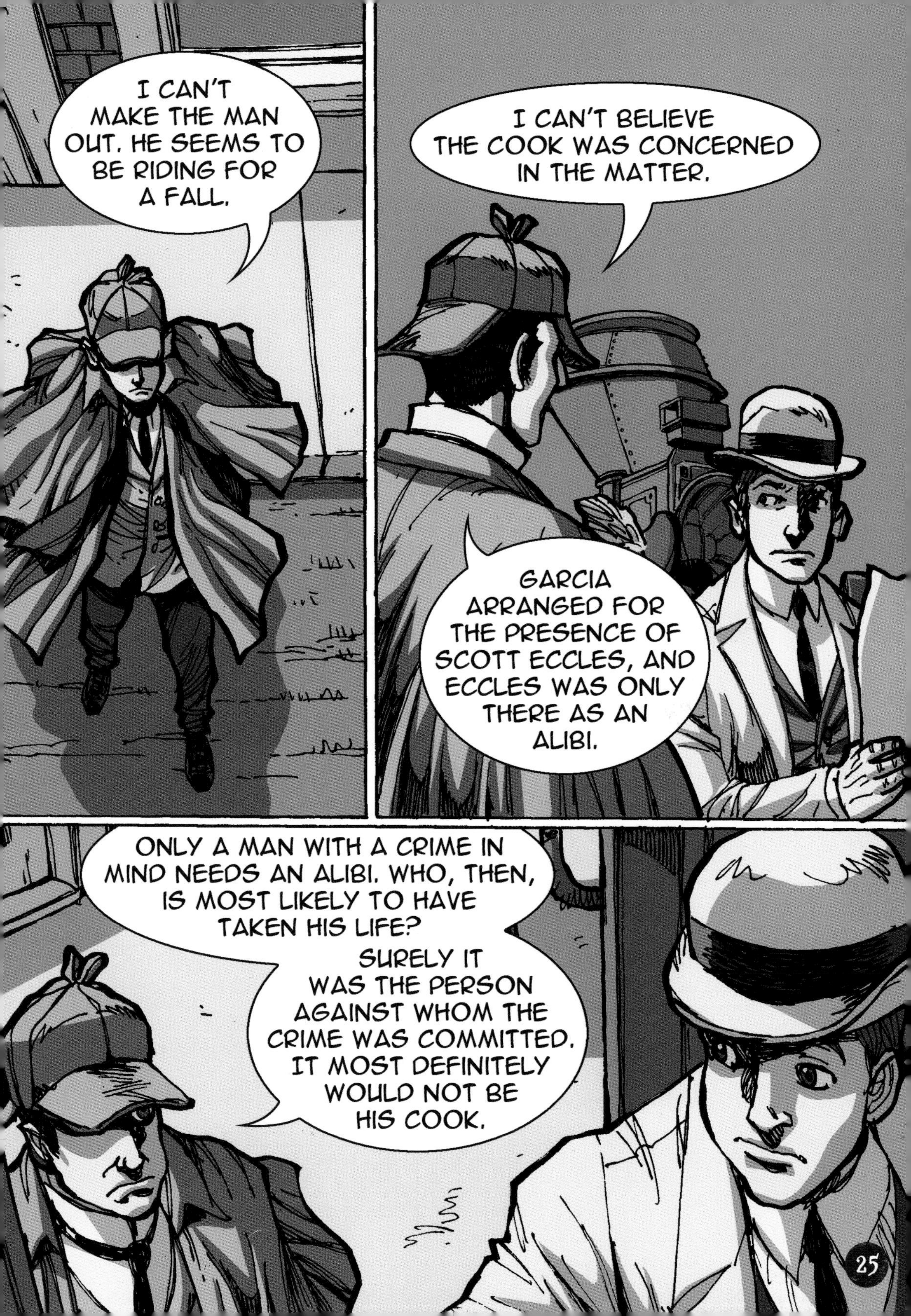
I CAN'T MAKE THE MAN OUT. HE SEEMS TO BE RIDING FOR A FALL.
I CAN'T BELIEVE THE COOK WAS CONCERNED IN THE MATTER.
GARCIA ARRANGED FOR THE PRESENCE OF SCOTT ECCLES, AND ECCLES WAS ONLY THERE AS AN ALIBI.
ONLY A MAN WITH A CRIME IN MIND NEEDS AN ALIBI. WHO, THEN, IS MOST LIKELY TO HAVE TAKEN HIS LIFE?
SURELY IT WAS THE PERSON AGAINST WHOM THE CRIME WAS COMMITTED. IT MOST DEFINITELY WOULD NOT BE HIS COOK.

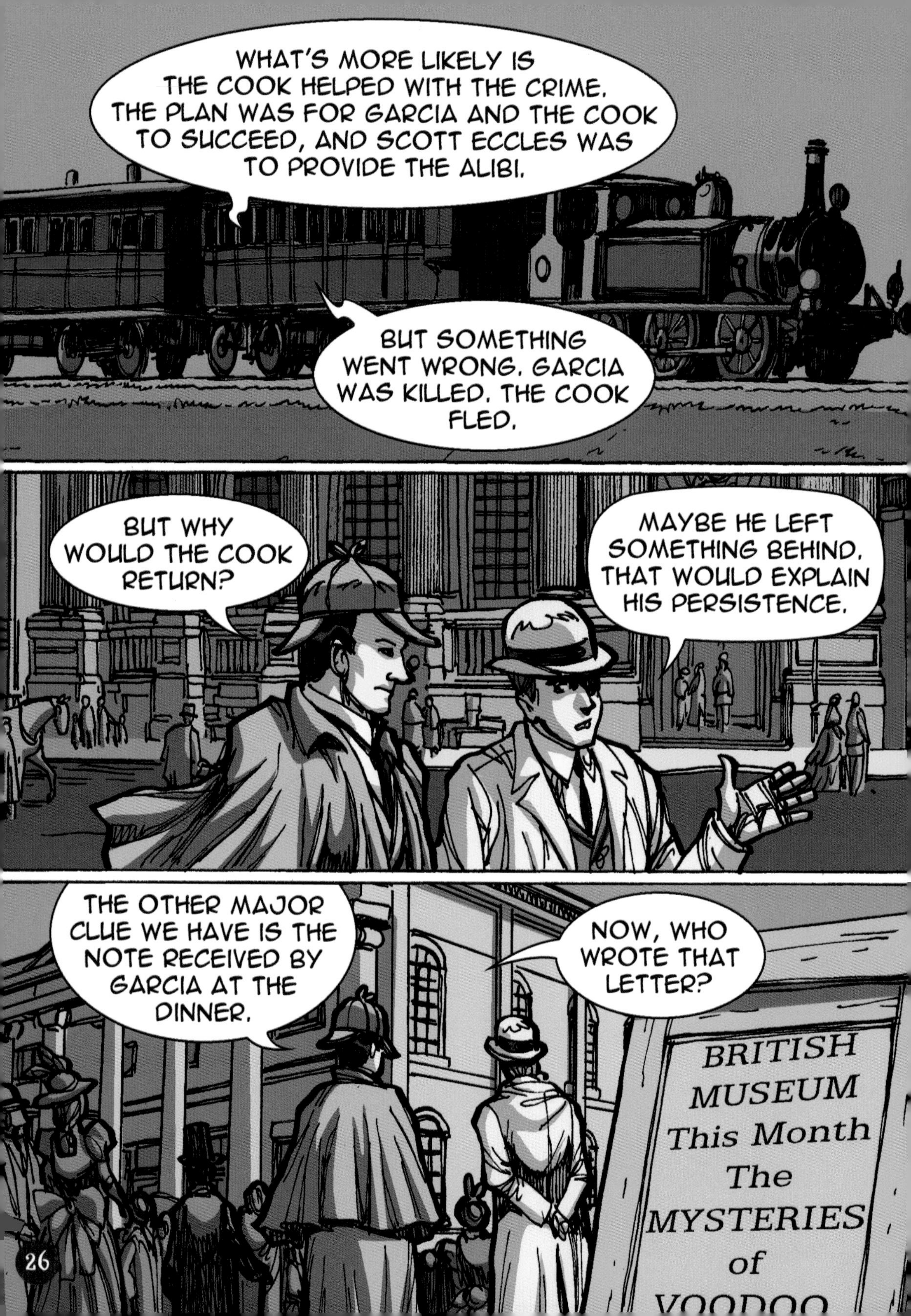
WHAT'S MORE LIKELY IS THE COOK HELPED WITH THE CRIME. THE PLAN WAS FOR GARCIA AND THE COOK TO SUCCEED, AND SCOTT ECCLES WAS TO PROVIDE THE ALIBI.
BUT SOMETHING WENT WRONG. GARCIA WAS KILLED. THE COOK FLED.
BUT WHY WOULD THE COOK RETURN?
MAYBE HE LEFT SOMETHING BEHIND. THAT WOULD EXPLAIN HIS PERSISTENCE.
THE OTHER MAJOR CLUE WE HAVE IS THE NOTE RECEIVED BY GARCIA AT THE DINNER.
NOW, WHO WROTE THAT LETTER?
BRITISH MUSEUM This Month The MYSTERIES of VOODOO

MOST OF THE HOUSES IN THE VILLAGE BELONG TO RESPECTABLE PEOPLE. BUT MR. HENDERSON OF HIGH GABLE IS A CURIOUS MAN TO WHOM ADVENTURES MIGHT BEFALL.

MR. HENDERSON IS EITHER A FOREIGNER OR HAS LIVED LONG IN THE TROPICS. HIS FRIEND AND SECRETARY, MR. LUCAS, IS UNDOUBTEDLY A FOREIGNER.

YOU SEE, WATSON, WE HAVE COME ALREADY UPON TWO SETS OF FOREIGNERS-- ONE AT WISTERIA LODGE AND ONE AT HIGH GABLE. OUR GAPS ARE BEGINNING TO CLOSE.

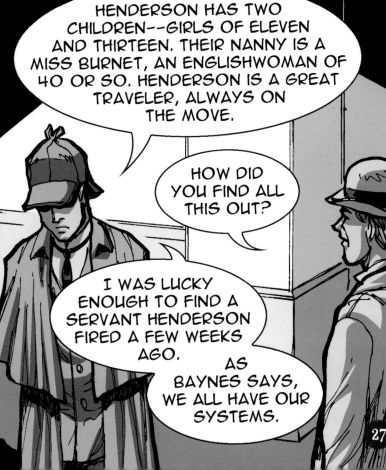

HENDERSON HAS TWO CHILDREN--GIRLS OF ELEVEN AND THIRTEEN. THEIR NANNY IS A MISS BURNET, AN ENGLISHWOMAN OF 40 OR SO. HENDERSON IS A GREAT TRAVELER, ALWAYS ON THE MOVE.

HOW DID YOU FIND ALL THIS OUT?

I CONCENTRATED MY ATTENTION, THEREFORE, UPON HIM AND HIS HOUSEHOLD.

I WAS LUCKY ENOUGH TO FIND A SERVANT HENDERSON FIRED A FEW WEEKS AGO.

AS BAYNES SAYS, WE ALL HAVE OUR SYSTEMS.

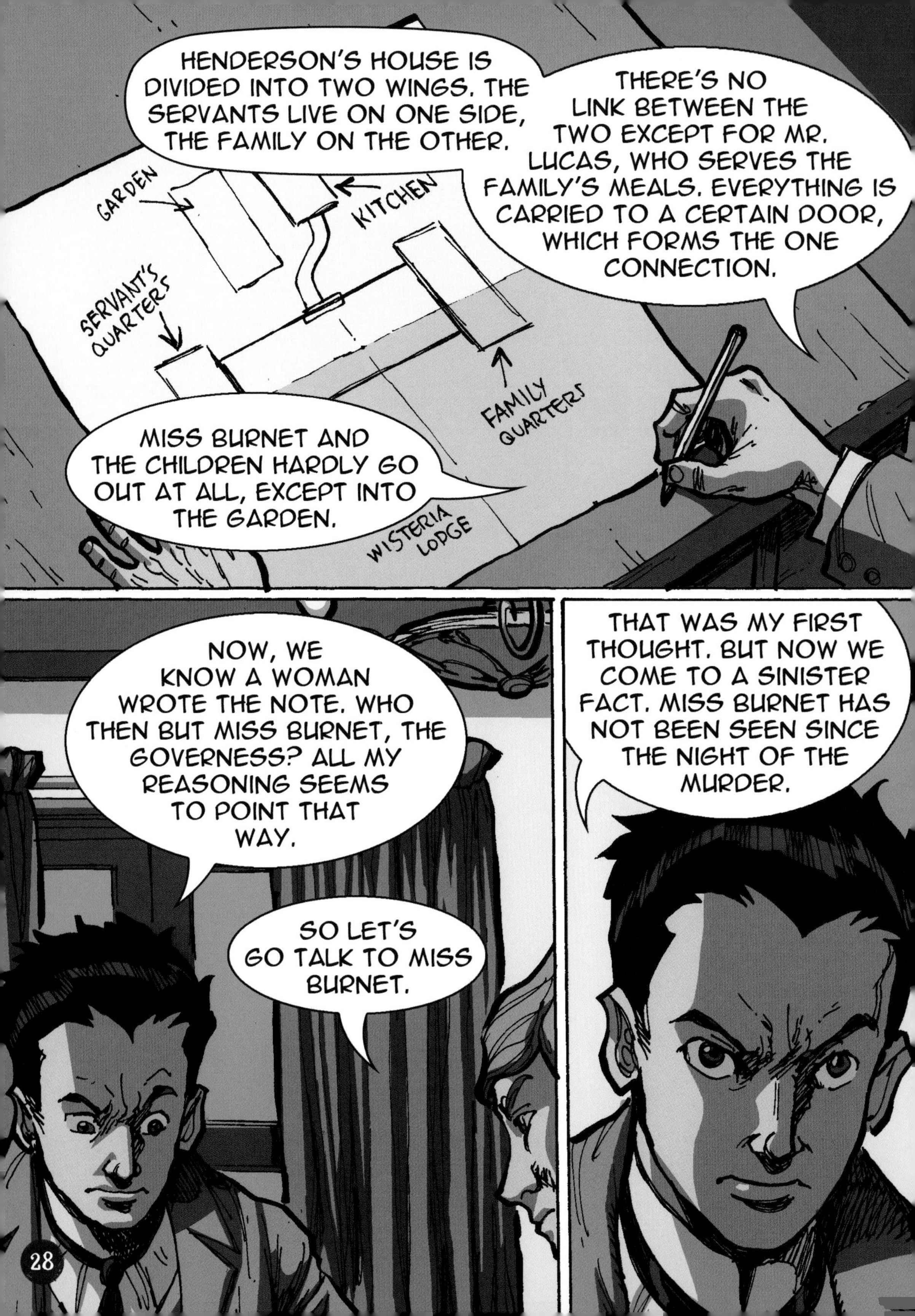
HENDERSON'S HOUSE IS DIVIDED INTO TWO WINGS. THE SERVANTS LIVE ON ONE SIDE, THE FAMILY ON THE OTHER.
THERE'S NO LINK BETWEEN THE TWO EXCEPT FOR MR. LUCAS, WHO SERVES THE FAMILY'S MEALS. EVERYTHING IS CARRIED TO A CERTAIN DOOR, WHICH FORMS THE ONE CONNECTION.
GARDEN
KITCHEN
SERVANT'S QUARTERS
FAMILY QUARTERS
MISS BURNET AND THE CHILDREN HARDLY GO OUT AT ALL, EXCEPT INTO THE GARDEN.
WISTERIA LODGE
NOW, WE KNOW A WOMAN WROTE THE NOTE. WHO THEN BUT MISS BURNET, THE GOVERNESS? ALL MY REASONING SEEMS TO POINT THAT WAY.
SO LET'S GO TALK TO MISS BURNET.
THAT WAS MY FIRST THOUGHT. BUT NOW WE COME TO A SINISTER FACT. MISS BURNET HAS NOT BEEN SEEN SINCE THE NIGHT OF THE MURDER.

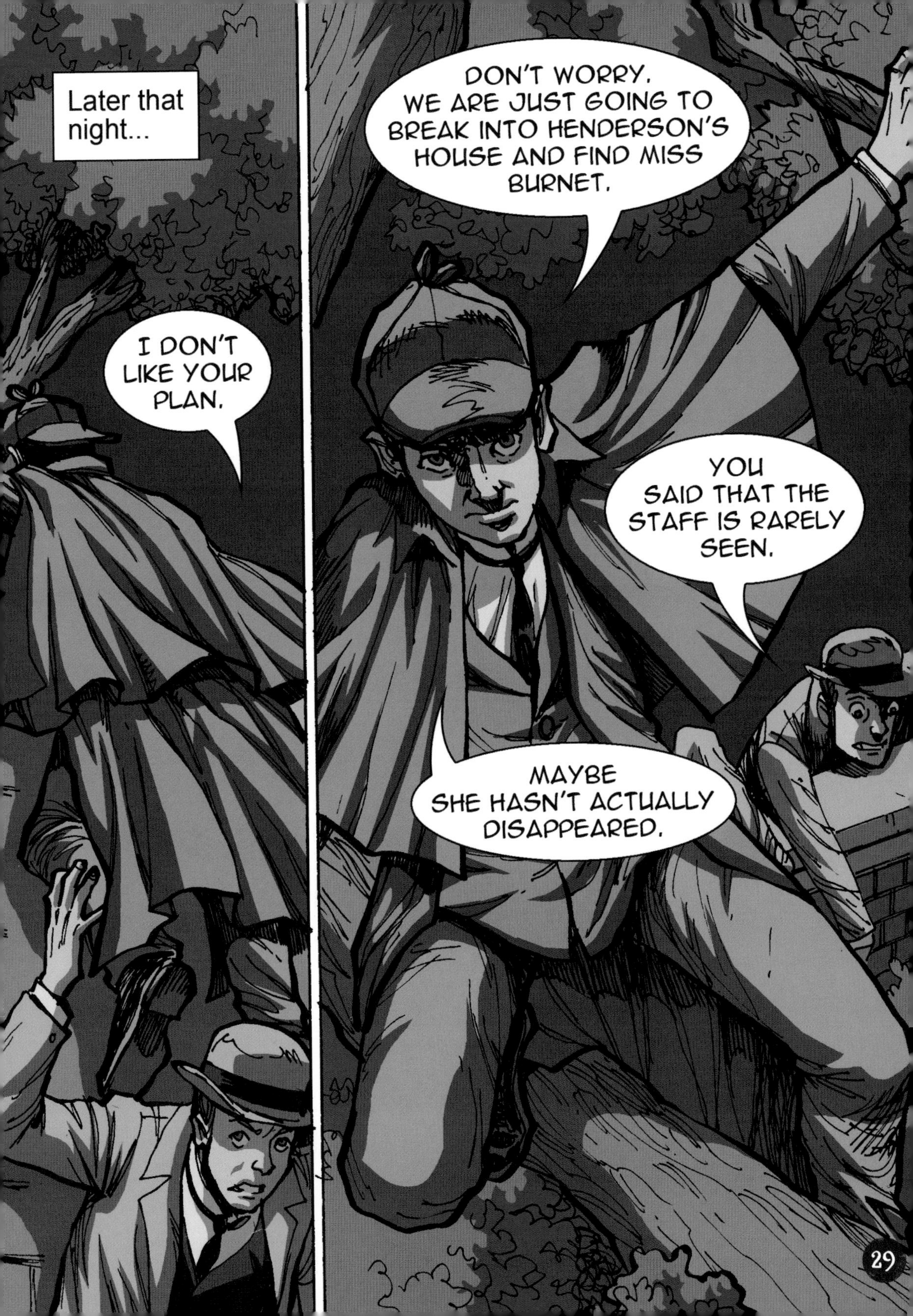
Later that night...
I DON'T LIKE YOUR PLAN.
DON'T WORRY. WE ARE JUST GOING TO BREAK INTO HENDERSON'S HOUSE AND FIND MISS BURNET.
YOU SAID THAT THE STAFF IS RARELY SEEN.
MAYBE SHE HASN'T ACTUALLY DISAPPEARED.

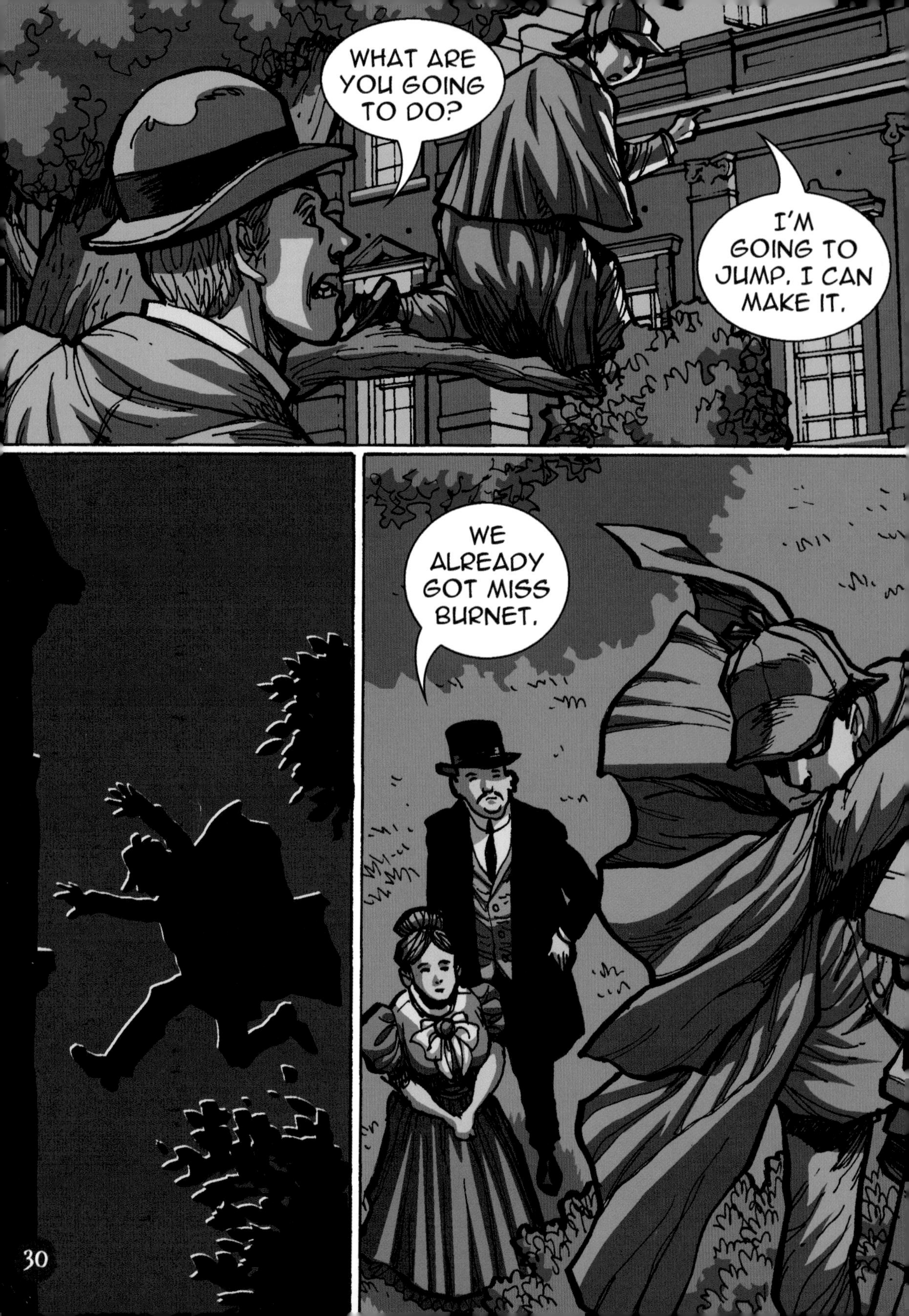
WHAT ARE YOU GOING TO DO?
I'M GOING TO JUMP. I CAN MAKE IT.
WE ALREADY GOT MISS BURNET.

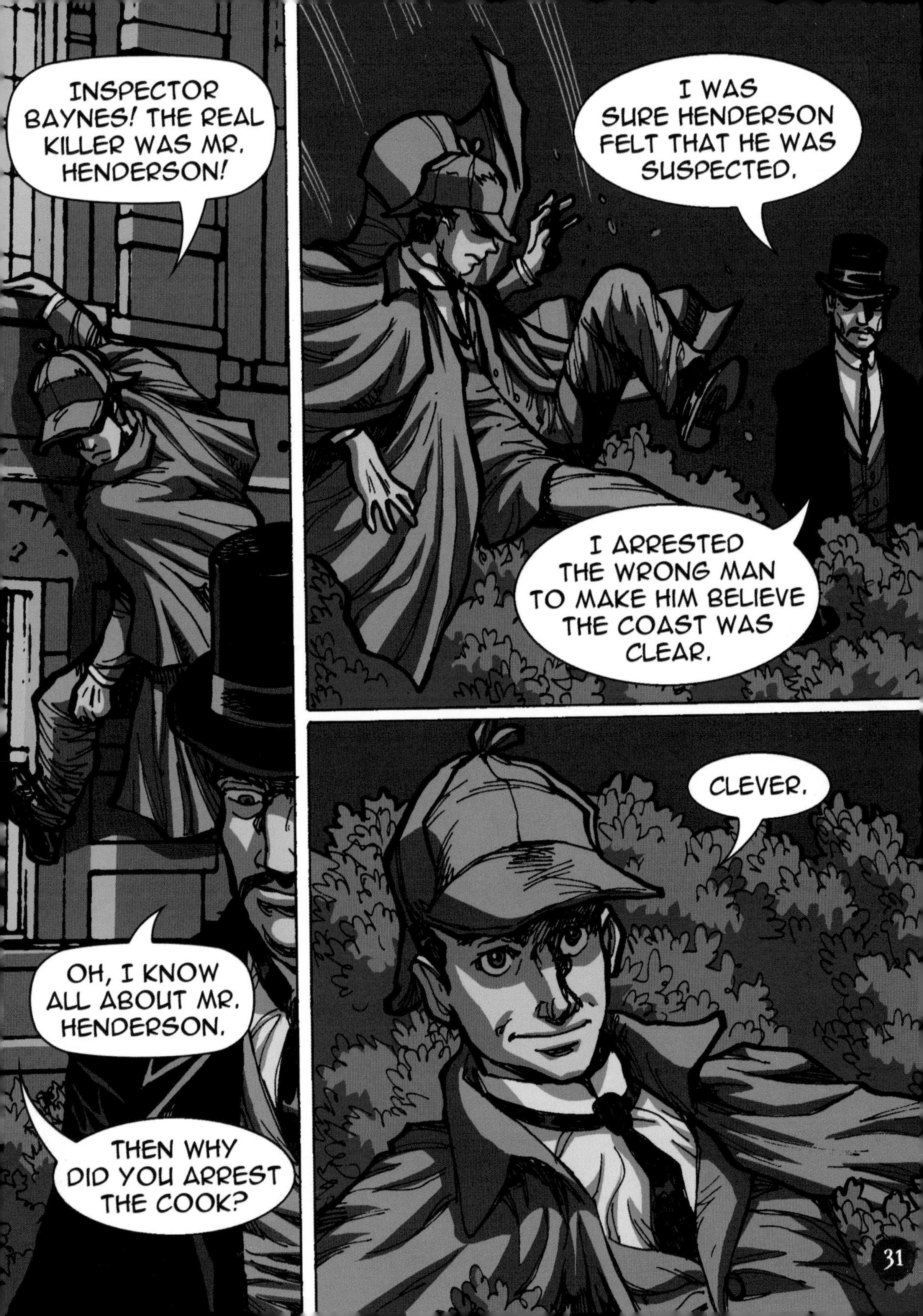
INSPECTOR BAYNES! THE REAL KILLER WAS MR. HENDERSON!
OH, I KNOW ALL ABOUT MR. HENDERSON.
THEN WHY DID YOU ARREST THE COOK?
I WAS SURE HENDERSON FELT THAT HE WAS SUSPECTED.
I ARRESTED THE WRONG MAN TO MAKE HIM BELIEVE THE COAST WAS CLEAR.
CLEVER.

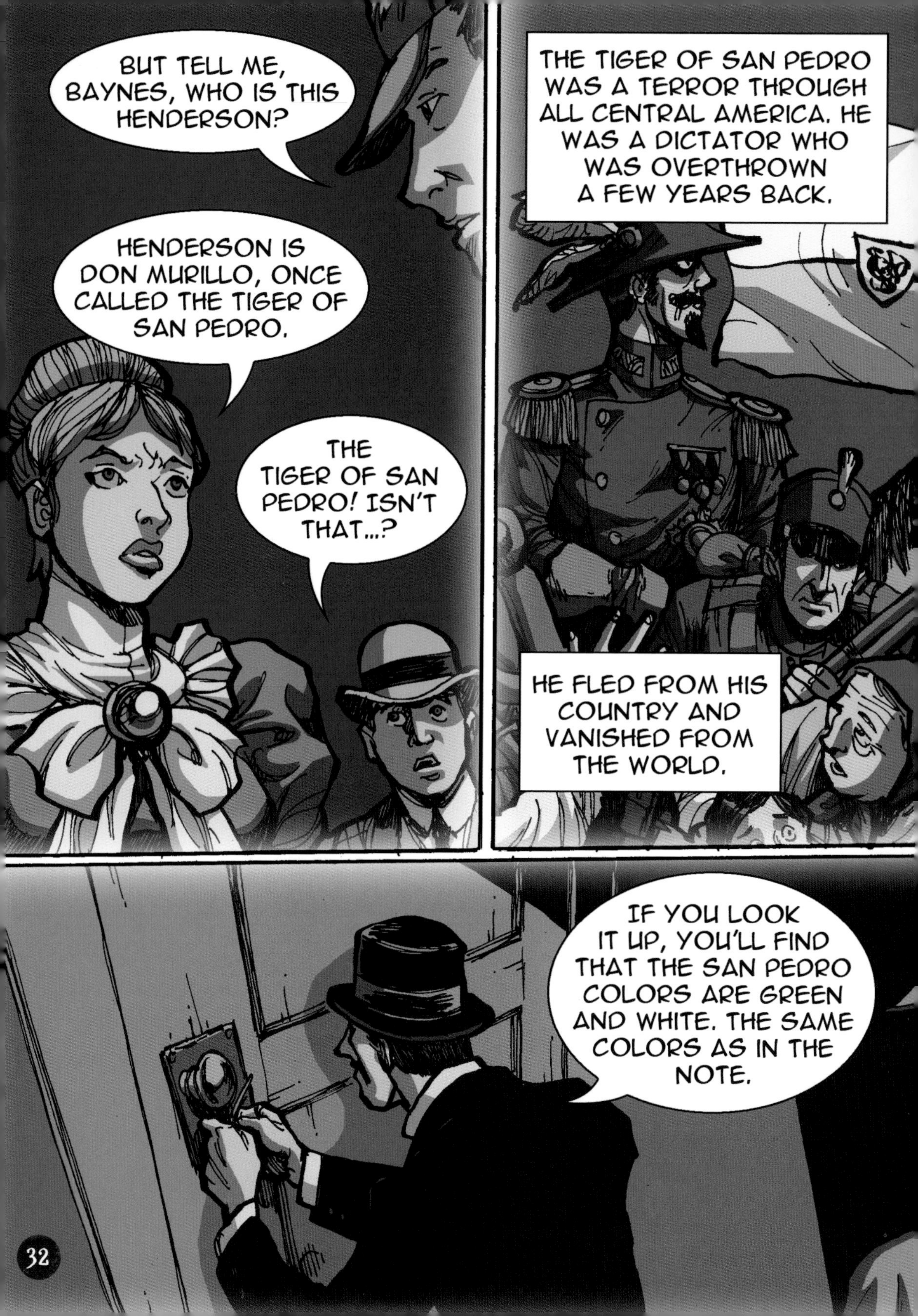
BUT TELL ME, BAYNES, WHO IS THIS HENDERSON?
HENDERSON IS DON MURILLO, ONCE CALLED THE TIGER OF SAN PEDRO.
THE TIGER OF SAN PEDRO! ISN'T THAT...?
THE TIGER OF SAN PEDRO WAS A TERROR THROUGH ALL CENTRAL AMERICA. HE WAS A DICTATOR WHO WAS OVERTHROWN A FEW YEARS BACK.
HE FLED FROM HIS COUNTRY AND VANISHED FROM THE WORLD.
IF YOU LOOK IT UP, YOU'LL FIND THAT THE SAN PEDRO COLORS ARE GREEN AND WHITE. THE SAME COLORS AS IN THE NOTE.

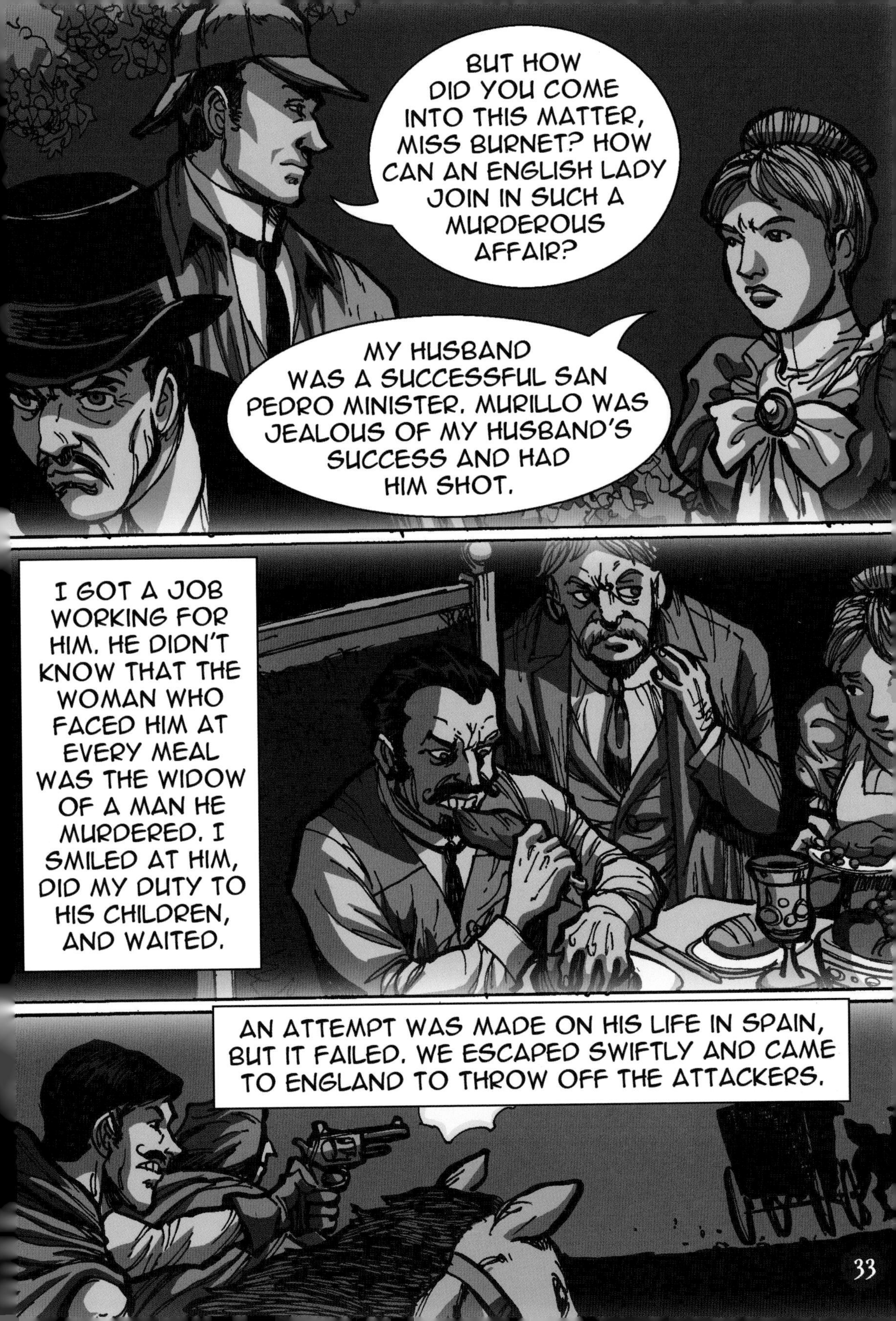
BUT HOW DID YOU COME INTO THIS MATTER, MISS BURNET? HOW CAN AN ENGLISH LADY JOIN IN SUCH A MURDEROUS AFFAIR?
MY HUSBAND WAS A SUCCESSFUL SAN PEDRO MINISTER. MURILLO WAS JEALOUS OF MY HUSBAND'S SUCCESS AND HAD HIM SHOT.
I GOT A JOB WORKING FOR HIM. HE DIDN'T KNOW THAT THE WOMAN WHO FACED HIM AT EVERY MEAL WAS THE WIDOW OF A MAN HE MURDERED. I SMILED AT HIM, DID MY DUTY TO HIS CHILDREN, AND WAITED.
AN ATTEMPT WAS MADE ON HIS LIFE IN SPAIN, BUT IT FAILED. WE ESCAPED SWIFTLY AND CAME TO ENGLAND TO THROW OFF THE ATTACKERS.

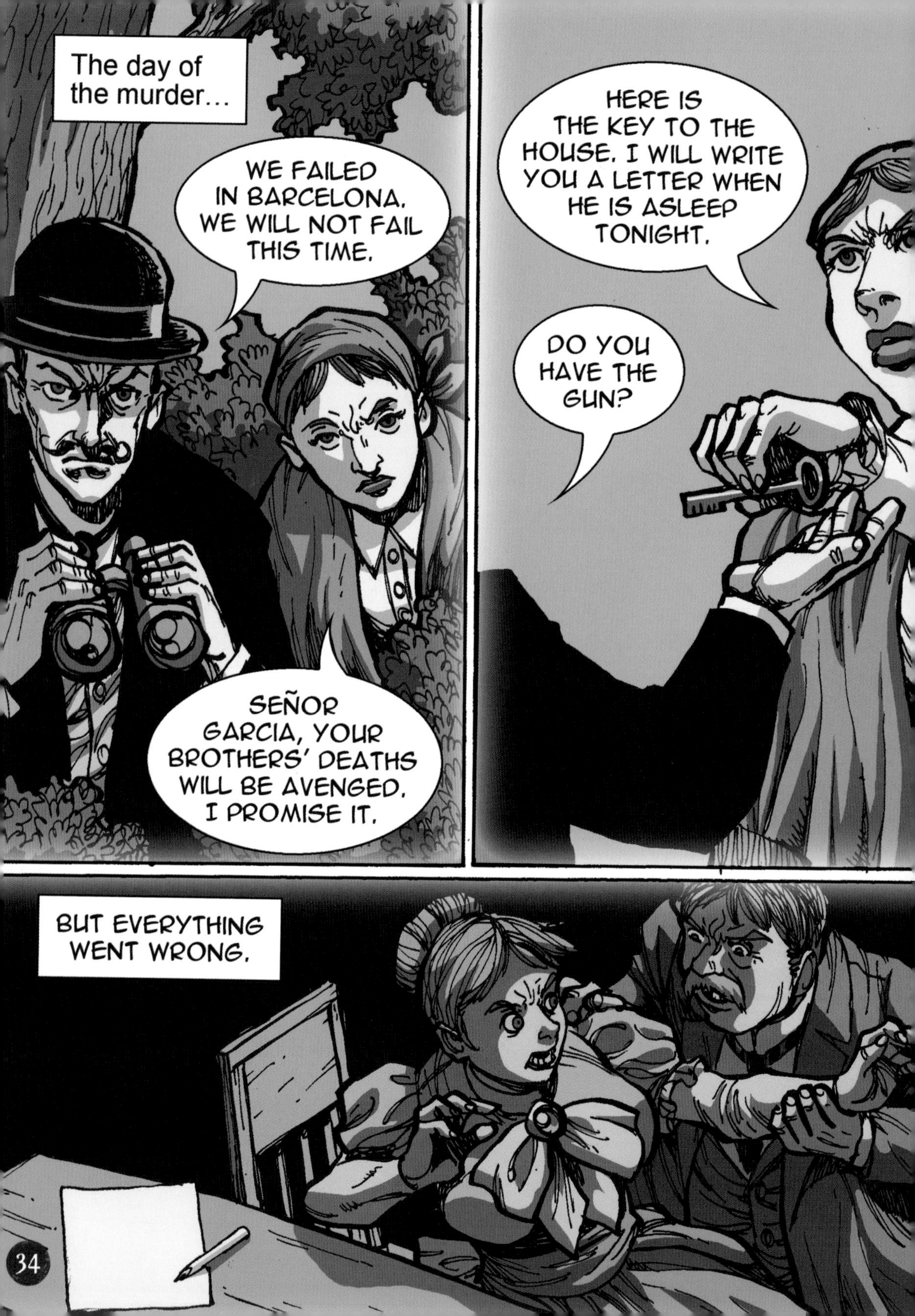
The day of the murder…
WE FAILED IN BARCELONA. WE WILL NOT FAIL THIS TIME.
SEÑOR GARCIA, YOUR BROTHERS' DEATHS WILL BE AVENGED. I PROMISE IT.
HERE IS THE KEY TO THE HOUSE. I WILL WRITE YOU A LETTER WHEN HE IS ASLEEP TONIGHT.
DO YOU HAVE THE GUN?
BUT EVERYTHING WENT WRONG.

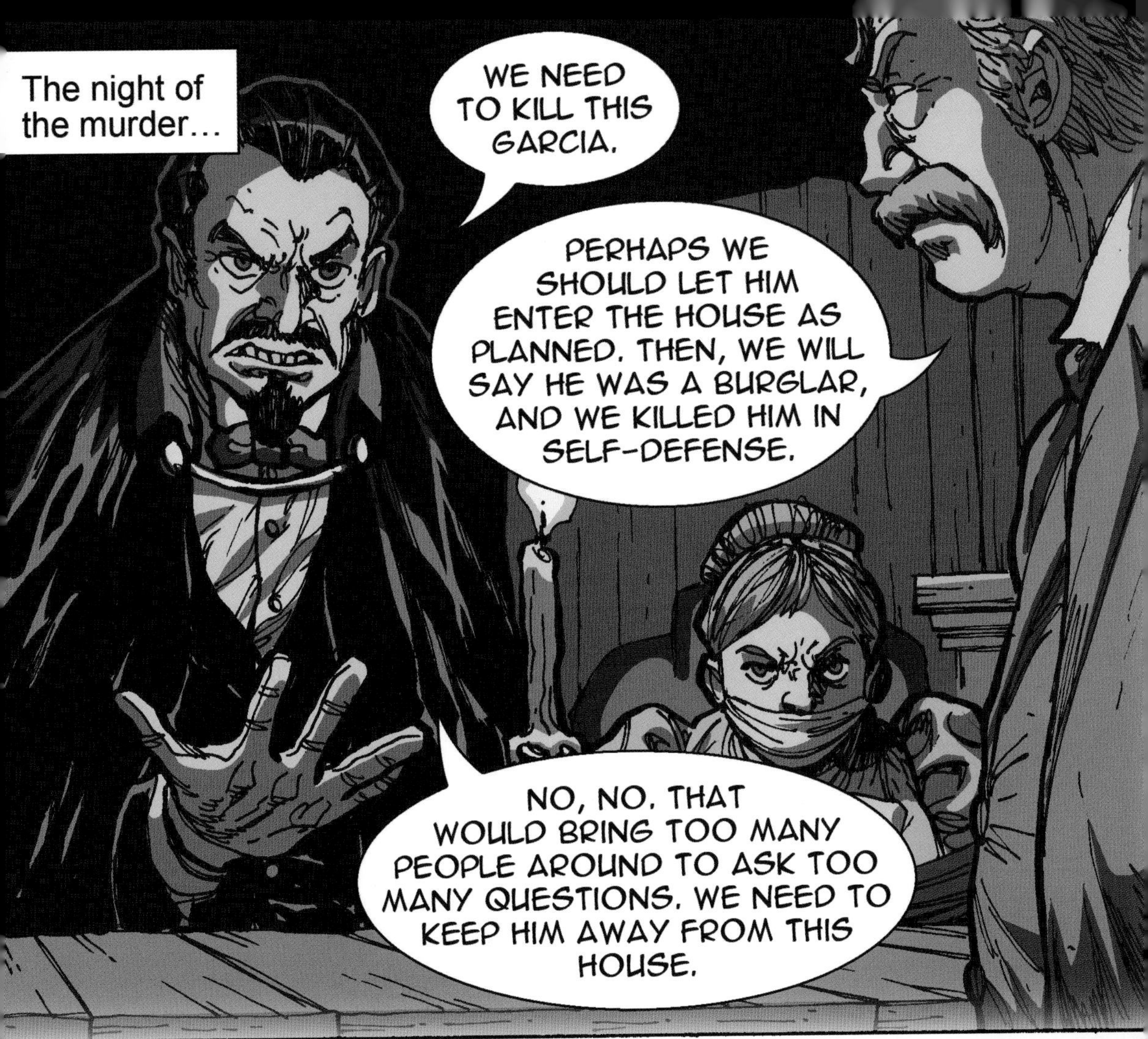
The night of the murder…
WE NEED TO KILL THIS GARCIA.
PERHAPS WE SHOULD LET HIM ENTER THE HOUSE AS PLANNED. THEN, WE WILL SAY HE WAS A BURGLAR, AND WE KILLED HIM IN SELF-DEFENSE.
NO, NO. THAT WOULD BRING TOO MANY PEOPLE AROUND TO ASK TOO MANY QUESTIONS. WE NEED TO KEEP HIM AWAY FROM THIS HOUSE.

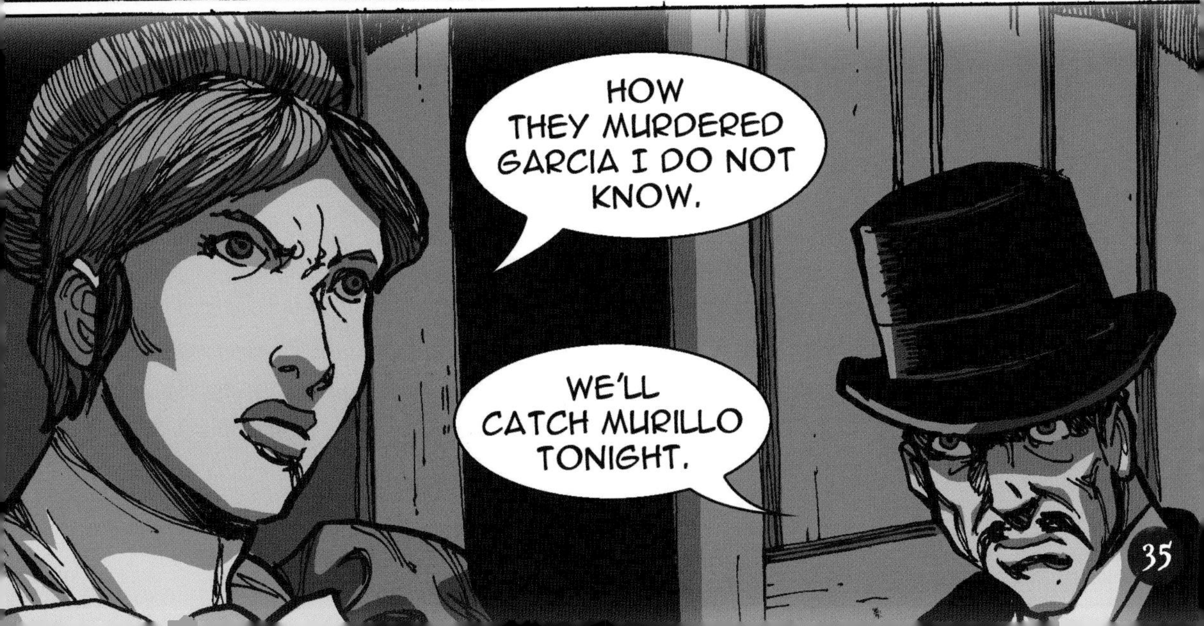
HOW THEY MURDERED GARCIA I DO NOT KNOW.
WE'LL CATCH MURILLO TONIGHT.

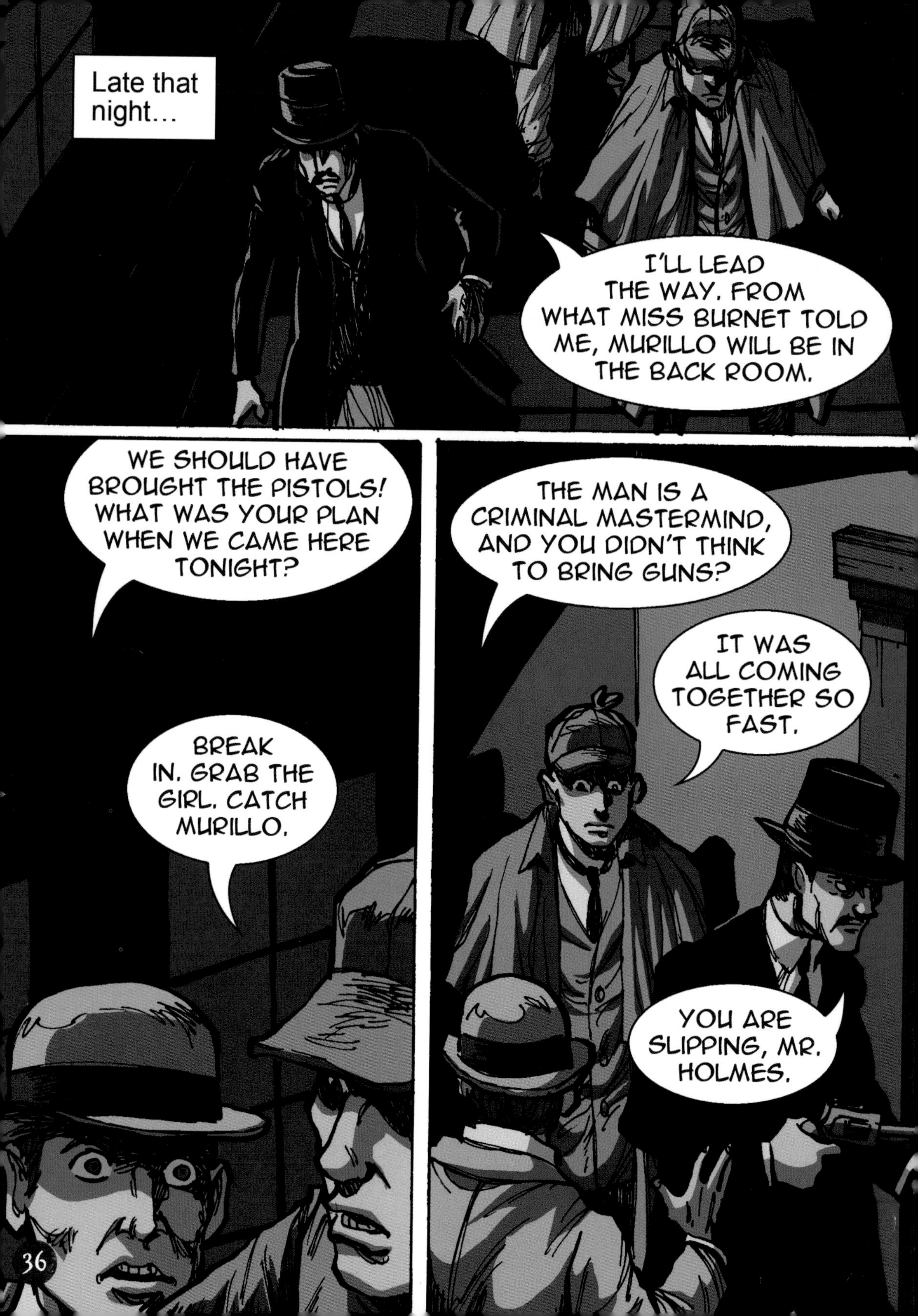
Late that night…
I'LL LEAD THE WAY. FROM WHAT MISS BURNET TOLD ME, MURILLO WILL BE IN THE BACK ROOM.
WE SHOULD HAVE BROUGHT THE PISTOLS! WHAT WAS YOUR PLAN WHEN WE CAME HERE TONIGHT?
BREAK IN. GRAB THE GIRL. CATCH MURILLO.
THE MAN IS A CRIMINAL MASTERMIND, AND YOU DIDN'T THINK TO BRING GUNS?
IT WAS ALL COMING TOGETHER SO FAST.
YOU ARE SLIPPING, MR. HOLMES.

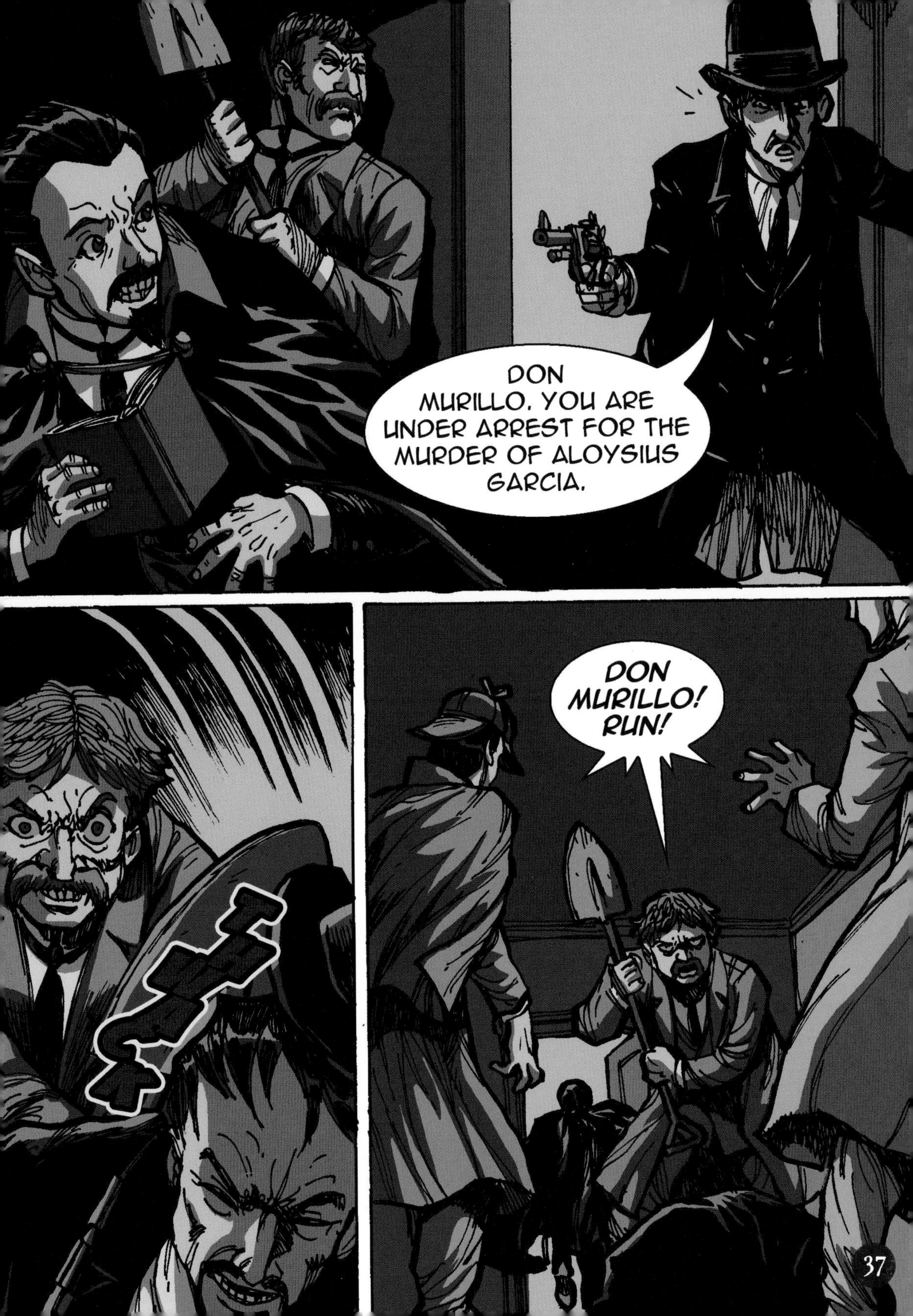
DON MURILLO. YOU ARE UNDER ARREST FOR THE MURDER OF ALOYSIUS GARCIA.
DON MURILLO! RUN!

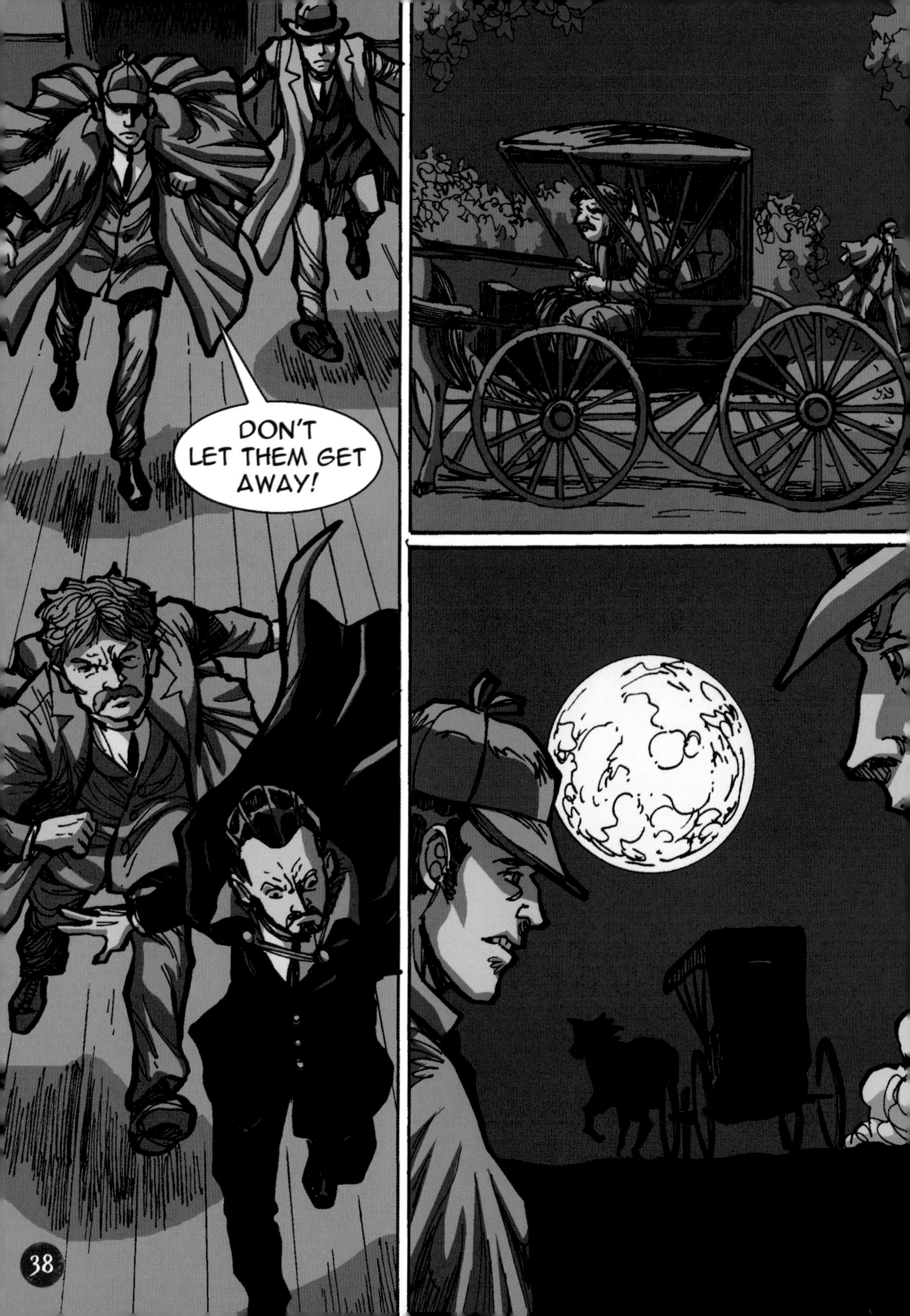
DON'T LET THEM GET AWAY!

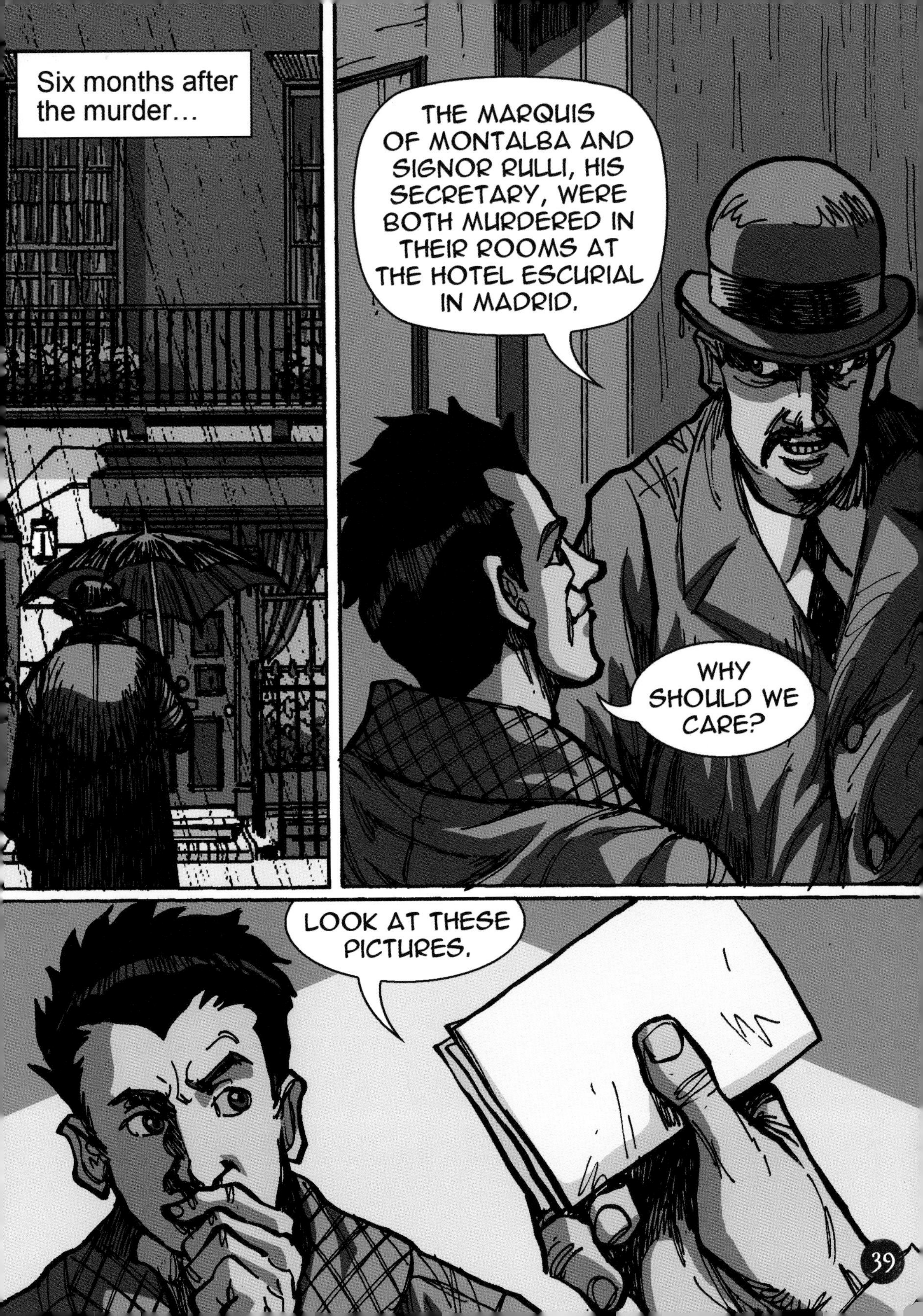
Six months after the murder…
THE MARQUIS OF MONTALBA AND SIGNOR RULLI, HIS SECRETARY, WERE BOTH MURDERED IN THEIR ROOMS AT THE HOTEL ESCURIAL IN MADRID.
WHY SHOULD WE CARE?
LOOK AT THESE PICTURES.

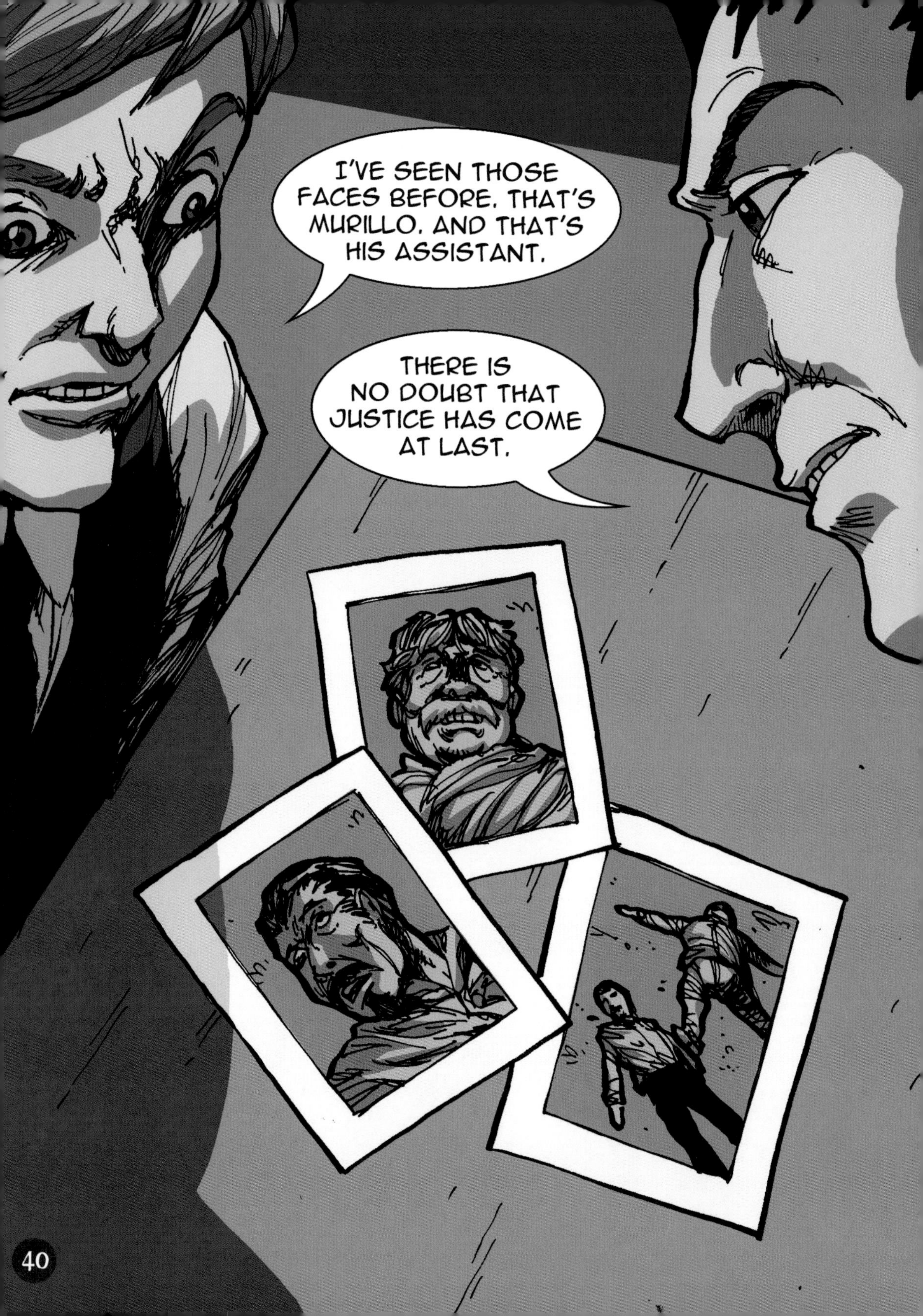
I'VE SEEN THOSE FACES BEFORE. THAT'S MURILLO. AND THAT'S HIS ASSISTANT.
THERE IS NO DOUBT THAT JUSTICE HAS COME AT LAST.

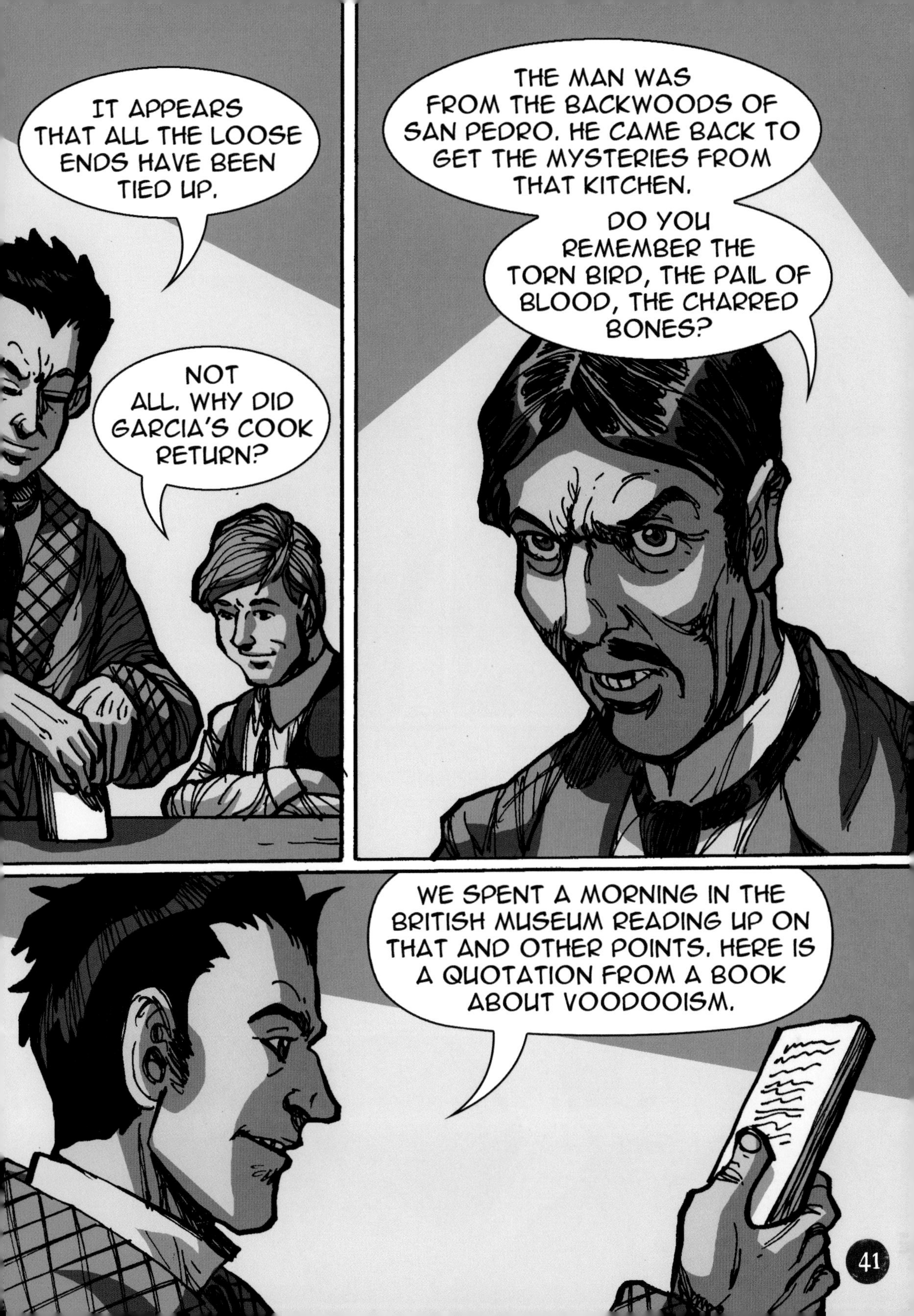
IT APPEARS THAT ALL THE LOOSE ENDS HAVE BEEN TIED UP.
NOT ALL. WHY DID GARCIA'S COOK RETURN?
THE MAN WAS FROM THE BACKWOODS OF SAN PEDRO. HE CAME BACK TO GET THE MYSTERIES FROM THAT KITCHEN.
DO YOU REMEMBER THE TORN BIRD, THE PAIL OF BLOOD, THE CHARRED BONES?
WE SPENT A MORNING IN THE BRITISH MUSEUM READING UP ON THAT AND OTHER POINTS. HERE IS A QUOTATION FROM A BOOK ABOUT VOODOOISM.

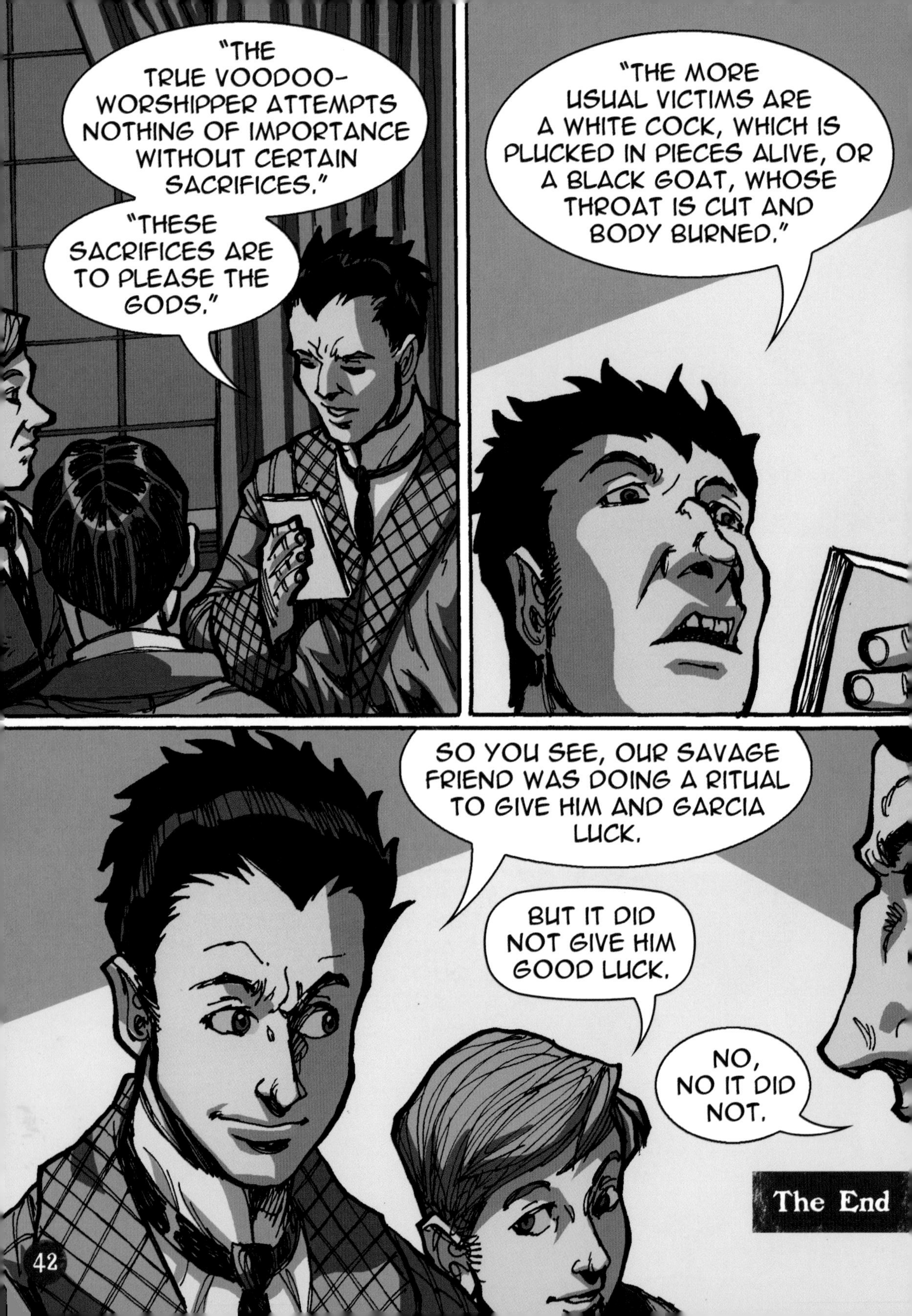
"THE TRUE VOODOO-WORSHIPPER ATTEMPTS NOTHING OF IMPORTANCE WITHOUT CERTAIN SACRIFICES."
"THESE SACRIFICES ARE TO PLEASE THE GODS."
"THE MORE USUAL VICTIMS ARE A WHITE COCK, WHICH IS PLUCKED IN PIECES ALIVE, OR A BLACK GOAT, WHOSE THROAT IS CUT AND BODY BURNED."
SO YOU SEE, OUR SAVAGE FRIEND WAS DOING A RITUAL TO GIVE HIM AND GARCIA LUCK.
BUT IT DID NOT GIVE HIM GOOD LUCK.
NO, NO IT DID NOT.
The End

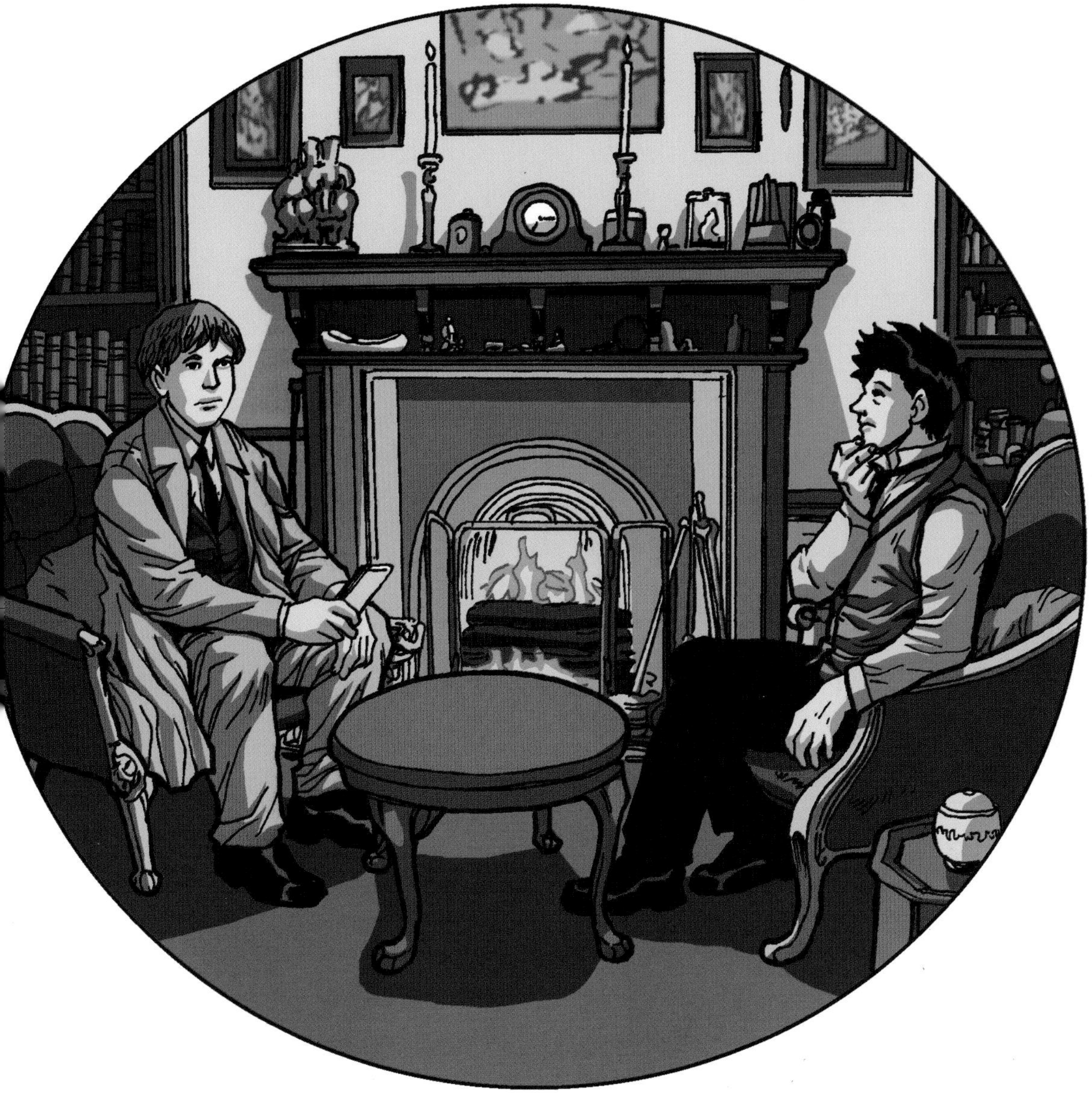

How to Draw
Sherlock Holmes
by Ben Dunn

Step 1: Use a pencil to draw a simple framework. You can start with a stick figure! Then add circles, ovals, and cylinders to get the basic form. Getting the simple shapes in place is the beginning to solving any great case.

Step 2: Time to add to Sherlock's look. Use the shapes you started with to fill in his clothes. Use guidelines to add circles for the eyes. And don't forget the hair.

Step 3: Now you can go in with a pen and start inking Sherlock. Fill in all the details and fix any mistakes. Let the ink dry to avoid smudges, then erase any pencil marks. Sherlock is ready for some color, so grab your markers and get started!

Glossary

accounting - the job of recording the amounts of money made and spent by a person or a business.

accusation - a statement that a person has committed a crime or an offense.

alibi - an excuse or proof of being somewhere else at the time of a crime to prove one is not guilty.

ambush - a surprise attack from a hidden position.

assassin - someone sent to murder a very important person, usually for political reasons.

avenge - to punish someone for the wrongs done to another person.

dictator - a ruler with complete control who usually governs in a cruel or unfair way.

disturb - to interfere with or interrupt.

embassy - the home and office of a diplomat who lives in a foreign country.

extraordinary - very unusual; special.

Godspeed - a send-off that wishes someone a prosperous journey.

mastermind - a person who is giving directions for a project.

persistence - the state of not giving up, even in difficulties.

presence - the state of being somewhere.

ritual - a form or order to a ceremony.

sinister - looking dangerous or evil.

voodoo - a religion often connected with magic and spells. It originated in western Africa.

whereabouts - the place where someone or something is.

Web Sites

To learn more about Sir Arthur Conan Doyle, visit ABDO Group online at **www.abdopublishing.com**. Web sites about Doyle are featured on our Book Links page. These links are routinely monitored and updated to provide the most current information available.

About the Author

Arthur Conan Doyle was born on May 22, 1859, in Edinburgh, Scotland. He was the second of Charles Altamont and Mary Foley Doyle's ten children. In 1868, Doyle began his schooling in England. Eight years later, he returned to Scotland.

Upon his return, Doyle entered the University of Edinburgh's medical school, where he became a doctor in 1885. That year, he married Louisa Hawkins. Together they had two children.

While a medical student, Doyle was impressed when his professor observed the tiniest details of a patient's condition. Doyle later wrote stories where his most famous character, Sherlock Holmes, used this same technique to solve mysteries. Holmes first appeared in *A Study in Scarlet* in 1887 and was immediately popular.

Between 1887 and 1927, Doyle wrote 66 stories and 3 novels about Holmes. He also wrote other fiction and nonfiction novels throughout his life. In 1902, Doyle was knighted for his work in a field hospital in the South African War. Four years later, Louisa died. Doyle married Jean Leckie in 1907, and they had three children together.

Sir Arthur Conan Doyle died on July 7, 1930, in Sussex, England. Today, Doyle's famous character, Sherlock Holmes, is honored with societies around the world that pay tribute to the detective.

Additional Works

A Study in Scarlet (1887)

The Mystery of Cloomber (1889)

The Firm of Girdlestone (1890)

The White Company (1891)

The Adventures of Sherlock Holmes (1891-92)

The Memoirs of Sherlock Holmes (1892-93)

Round the Red Lamp (1894)

The Stark Munro Letters (1895)

The Great Boer War (1900)

The Hound of the Baskervilles (1901-02)

The Return of Sherlock Holmes (1903-04)

Through the Magic Door (1907)

The Crime of the Congo (1909)

The Coming of the Fairies (1922)

Memories and Adventures (1924)

The Case-Book of Sherlock Holmes (1921-27)

About the Adapters

Author

Vincent Goodwin earned his BA in Drama and Communications from Trinity University in San Antonio. He is the writer of three plays as well as the cowriter of the comic book *Pirates vs. Ninjas II*. Goodwin is also an accomplished journalist, having won several awards for his work as a columnist and reporter.

Illustrator

Ben Dunn founded Antarctic Press, one of the largest comic companies in the United States. His works appear in Marvel and Image comics. He is best known for his series *Ninja High School* and *Warrior Nun Areala*.